A manuscript from a Conservatoire of Music

Sirs, it may have come to your notice that in music we have a term '*Scotch Snap*'. This usually takes the form of a semiquaver followed by a dotted quaver, a device favoured particularly by baroque composers such as Handel giving a distinctive 'jerky' character to a dance tune.

It has been suggested in the Professors' Common Room that this figure derived its name from the rough liquors of the time which imparted *a sudden jolt to the Scottish tastebuds.*

Today, of course, we have The Macallan Single Highland Malt Whisky, which provides such a delectable legato that the *Scotch* snap has become quite forgotten – except of course in those bars where only baser spirits are jiggered out (in which case, may we suggest a *bar's rest?*).

Yours etc., Ian Curror,

FRCO (CHM), GRSM, ARCM, LRAM *and BAR.*

THE MACALLAN. THE MALT.

THE MACALLAN® Scotch Whisky. 43% alc./vol. Sole U.S. importer Rémy Amerique, Inc., New York, N.Y.

The Paris Review

The Paris Review is published quarterly by The Paris Review, Inc. Vol. 40, No. 149, Winter 1998. Business Office: 45-39 171st Place, Flushing, New York 11358 (ISSN #0031-2037). Paris Office: Harry Mathews, 67 rue de Grenelle, Paris 75007 France. London Office: Shusha Guppy, 8 Shawfield St., London, SW3. US distributors: Random House, Inc. 1(800)733-3000. Typeset and printed in USA by Capital City Press, Montpelier, VT. Price for single issue in USA: $10.00. $14.00 in Canada. Post-paid subscription for four issues $34.00, lifetime subscription $1000. Postal surcharge of $10.00 per four issues outside USA (excluding life subscriptions). Subscription card is bound within magazine. Please give six weeks notice of change of address using subscription card. *While The Paris Review welcomes the submission of unsolicited manuscripts, it cannot accept responsibility for their loss or delay, or engage in related correspondence. Manuscripts will not be returned or responded to unless accompanied by self-addressed, stamped envelope. Fiction manuscripts should be submitted to George Plimpton, poetry to Richard Howard, The Paris Review, 541 East 72nd Street, New York, N.Y. 10021.* Charter member of the Council of Literary Magazines and Presses. This publication is made possible, in part, with public funds from the New York State Council on the Arts and the National Endowment for the Arts. Periodicals postage paid at Flushing, New York, and at additional mailing offices. **Postmaster:** Please send address changes to 45-39 171st Place, Flushing, N.Y. 11358.

The Paris Review

Editorial Office:
541 East 72 Street
New York, New York 10021
HTTP://www.parisreview.com

Business & Circulation:
45-39 171 Place
Flushing, New York 11358

Distributed by Random House
201 East 50 Street
New York, N.Y. 10022
(800) 733-3000

Table of contents illustration by Richard Basil Mock, untitled linoblock.
Frontispiece by William Pène du Bois.

Number 149

When She Is Old and I Am Famous

Julie Orringer

There are grape leaves, like a crown, on her head. Grapes hang in her hair, and in her hands she holds the green vines. She dances with both arms in the air. On her smallest toe she wears a ring of pink shell.

Can someone tell her, please, to go home? This is my Italy and my story. We are in a vineyard near Florence. I have just turned twenty. She is a girl, a gangly teen, and she is a model. She is famous for almost getting killed. Last year, when she was fifteen, a photographer asked her to dance on the rail of a bridge and she fell. A metal rod beneath the water pierced her chest. Water came into the wound, close to her heart, and for three weeks she was in the hospital with an infection so furious it made her chant nonsense. All the while she got thinner and more pale, until, when she emerged, they thought she might be the best model there ever was. Her hair is wavy and long and buckeye-brown, and her blue eyes have a stunned, sad look to them. She is five feet eleven inches tall and weighs one hundred and thirteen pounds. She has told me so.

This week she is visiting from Paris, where she lives with her father, my Uncle Claude. When Claude was a young man he left college to become the darling of a great couturier, who introduced him to the sequin-and-powder world of Paris drag. Monsieur M. paraded my uncle around in black-and-white evening gowns, high-heeled pumps and sprayed-up diva hairdos. I have seen pictures in his attic back in Fernald, Indiana, my uncle leaning over some balustrade in a cloud of pink chiffon, silk roses at his waist. One time he appeared in *Vogue*, in a couture photo spread. All this went on for years, until I was six, when a postcard came asking us to pick him up at the Chicago airport. He came off the plane holding a squirming baby. Neither my mother nor I knew anything about his having a child, or even a female lover. Yet there she was, my infant cousin, and here she is now, in the vineyard doing her grape-leaf dance for my friends and me.

Aïda. That is her terrible name. *Ai-ee-duh*: two cries of pain and one of stupidity. The vines tighten around her body as she spins, and Joseph snaps photographs. She knows he will like it, the way the leaves cling, and the way the grapes stain her white dress. We are trespassing here in a vintner's vines, spilling the juice of his expensive grapes, and if he sees us here he will surely shoot us. What an end to my tall little cousin. Between the purple stains on her chest, a darker stain spreads. Have I mentioned yet that I am fat?

Isn't it funny, how I've learned to say it? I am fat. I am not skin or muscle or gristle or bone. What I am, the part of my body that I most am, is fat. Continuous, white, lighter than water, a source of energy. No one can hold all of me at once. Does this constitute a crime? I know how to carry myself. Sometimes I feel almost graceful. But all around I hear the thin people's bombast: *Get Rid of Flabby Thighs Now! Avoid Holiday Weight-Gain Nightmares! Lose Those Last Five Pounds!* What is left of a woman once her last five pounds are gone?

I met Drew and Joseph in my drawing class in Florence. Joseph is a blond sculptor from Manhattan, and Drew is a thirty-seven-year-old painter from Wisconsin. In drawing class we had neighboring easels, and Drew and I traded roll-eyed glances over Joe's loud Walkman. We both found ourselves drawing in techno-rhythm. When we finally complained to him, he told us he started wearing it because Drew and I talked too much. I wish that were true. I hardly talk to anyone, even after three months in Florence.

One evening as the three of us walked home from class we passed a billboard showing Cousin Aïda in a gray silk gown, and when I told them she was my cousin they both laughed as if I had made some sort of feminist comment. I insisted that I was telling the truth. That was a mistake. They sat me down at a café and made me talk about her for half an hour. Joseph wondered whether she planned to complete her schooling or follow her career, and Drew had to know whether she suffered from eating disorders and skewed self-esteem. It would have been easier if they'd just stood in front of the billboard and drooled. At least I would have been able to anticipate their mute stupor when they actually met her.

Aïda rolls her shoulders and lets her hair fall forward, hiding her face in shadow. They can't take their eyes off her. Uncle Claude would scold her for removing her sun hat. I have picked it up and am wearing it now. It is gold straw and it fits perfectly. What else of hers could I put on? Not even her gloves.

"Now stand perfectly still," Joseph says, extending his thumb and index finger as if to frame her. He snaps a few pictures then lets the camera drop. He looks as if he would like to throw a net over her. He will show these pictures of Aïda to his friends back home, telling them how he slept with her between the grapevines. This will be a lie, I hope. "Dance again," he says, "this time slower."

She rotates her hips like a Balinese dancer. "Like this?"

"That's it," he says. "Nice and slow." Surreptitiously he adjusts his shorts.

When Drew looks at my cousin I imagine him taking notes for future paintings. In Wisconsin he works as a professional muralist, and here he is the best drawing student in our class, good even at representing the foot when it faces forward. I am hopeless at drawing the foot at any angle. My models all look like they are sliding off the page. I've seen photographs of Drew's murals, twenty-foot-high paintings on the sides of elementary schools and parking structures, and his figures look as though they could step out of the wall and crush your car. He does paintings of just the feet. I can tell he's studying Aïda's pink toes right now. Later he will draw her, at night in his room, while his upstairs neighbor practices the violin until the crack of dawn. "If she didn't live there, I'd have to hire her to live there," he tells me. She may keep him up all night, but at least she makes him paint well.

There are certain things I can never abide: lack of food, lack of sleep and Aïda. But she is here in Italy on my free week because our parents thought it would be fun for us. "Aïda doesn't get much rest," my mother told me. "She needs time away from that business in France."

I told my mother that Aïda made me nervous. "Her name has an umlaut, for crying out loud."

"She's your cousin," my mother said.

"She's been on the covers of twelve magazines."

"Well, Mira"—and here her voice became sweet, almost reverent—"you are a future Michelangelo."

There's no question about my mother's faith in me. She has always believed I will succeed, never once taking into account my failure to represent the human figure. She says I have a "style." That may be true, but it does not make me the next anybody. Sometimes I freeze in front of the canvas, full of the knowledge that if I keep painting, sooner or later I will fail her.

My cousin always knew how important she was, even when she was little. Over at her house in Indiana I had to watch her eat ice-cream bars while I picked at my Sunmaid raisins. I tried to be nice because my mother had said, "Be nice." I told her she had a pretty name, that I knew she was named after a character from a Verdi opera, which my mom and I had listened to all the way from Chicago to Indiana. Aïda licked the chocolate from around her lips, then folded the silver wrapper. "I'm not named after the *character*," she said. "I'm named after the *entire opera.*"

The little bitch is a prodigy, a skinny Venus, a genius. She knows how to shake it. She will never be at a loss for work or money. She is a human dollar sign. Prada has made millions on her. And still her eyes remain clear and she gets enough sleep at night.

Joseph has run out of film. "You have beautiful teeth," he says hopelessly.

She grins for him.

Drew looks at me and shakes his head, and I am thankful.

When she's tired of the dance, Aïda untwines the vines from her body and lets them fall to the ground. She squashes a plump grape between her toes, looking into the distance. Then, as though compelled by some sign in the sky, she climbs to the top of a ridge and looks down into the valley. Joseph and Drew follow to see what she sees, and I have no choice but to follow as well. Where the vines end, the land slopes down into a bowl of dry grass. Near its center, surrounded by overgrown hedges and flower beds, the vintner's house rises, a sprawling two-story villa with a crumbling tile roof. Aïda inhales and turns toward the three of us, her eyes steady. "That's where my mother lives," she announces.

It is such an astounding lie, I cannot even bring myself to respond. Aïda's mother was the caterer at a party Uncle Claude attended during his "wild years;" my own mother related the story to me years ago as a cautionary tale. When Aïda was eight weeks old her mother left her with Claude, and that was that. But Aïda's tone is earnest and forthright, and both Joseph and Drew look up, confused.

"I thought you lived with your dad in Paris," Joseph says. He shoots a hard glance at me as if I've been concealing her whereabouts all this time.

"She does," I say.

Aïda shrugs. "My mother's family owns this whole place."

"This is news." Joseph looks at me, and I shake my head.

"My mom and I aren't very close," Aïda says and sits down. She ties a piece of grass into a knot, then tosses it down the hill. "Actually, the last time I saw her I was three." She draws her legs up and hugs her knees, and her shoulders rise and fall as she sighs. "It's not the kind of thing you do in Italy, tote around your bastard kid. It would have been a *vergogna* to the *famiglia*, as they say."Aïda looks down at the stone house in the valley.

Joseph and Drew exchange a glance, seeming to decide how to handle this moment. I find myself wordless. It's true that Aïda's mother didn't want to raise her. I don't doubt that it would have been a disgrace to her Catholic family. What baffles me is how Aïda can make up this story when she knows that *I* know it's bullshit. What does she expect will happen? Does she think I'll pretend to believe her? Joseph's eyebrows draw together with concern. I can't tell what he's thinking.

Aïda stands and dusts her hands against her dress, then begins to make her way down the slope. Joe gives us a look, shakes his head as if ashamed of himself, and then follows her.

"Where the hell do you think you're going?" I call to Aïda.

She turns, and the wind lifts her hair like a pennant. Her chin is set hard. "I'm going to get something from her," she says. "I'm not going back to France without a memento."

"Let's stop this now, Aïda," I say. "You're not related to anyone who lives in that house." In fact, it didn't look as if anyone lived there at all. The garden was a snarl of overgrown bushes, and the windows looked blank like sightless eyes.

"Go home," she says. "Joe will come with me. And don't pretend you're worried. If I didn't come back, you'd be glad."

She turns away and I watch her descend toward the villa, my tongue dry in my mouth.

These past days Aïda has been camping on my bedroom floor. Asleep she looks like a collapsed easel, something hard and angular lying where it shouldn't. Yesterday morning I opened one eye to see her fingering the contents of a blue tin box, my private cache of condoms. When I sat up and pushed the mosquito netting aside, she shoved the box back under the bed.

"What are you doing?" I asked.

The color rose in her cheeks.

"It's none of my business," I said. "But if you meet a guy."

She gave an abbreviated "ha" like the air had been punched out of her. Then she got up and began to look for something in her suitcase. Very quietly she said, "Of course, you're the expert."

"What's that supposed to mean?" I said.

She turned around and smiled with just her lips. "Nothing."

"Listen, shitweed, I may not be the next *Vogue* cover girl, but that doesn't mean I sleep alone every night."

"Whatever you say." She shook out a teeny dress and held it against herself.

"For God's sake," I said. "Do you have to be primo bitch of the whole universe?"

She tilted her head, coy and intimate. "You know what I think, Mira?" she said. "I think you're a vibrator cowgirl. I think you're riding the mechanical bull."

I had nothing to say. But something flew at her and I knew I had thrown it. She ducked. A glass candlestick broke against the wall.

"Fucking psycho!" she shouted. "Are you trying to kill me?"

"Get a hotel room," I said. "You're not staying here."

"Fine with me. I'll sleep in a ditch and you can sleep alone."

Her tone was plain and hard, eggshell white, but for a split second her lower lip quivered. It occurred to me for the first time that she might feel shunted off, that she might see me as a kind of baby-sitter she had to abide while her father had a break from her. Quickly I tried to replay in my mind all the names she had called me, that day and throughout our kid years, so I could shut out any thoughts that would make me feel sorry for her. "Get out of my room," I said. She picked her way across the glass and went into the bathroom. Door-click, faucet-knob squeak and then her scream, because in my apartment there is no hot water to be had, ever, by anyone.

Drew and I shuffle sideways down a rock hill toward the dried-up garden. Fifty yards below, my cousin sidles along the wall of the house. I cannot imagine how she plans to enter this fortress or what she will say if someone sees her. There's a rustle in a bank of hedges, and we see Joseph creeping along, his camera bag banging against his leg. He disappoints me. Back in New York he works in a fashion photographer's darkroom, and he speaks of commercial photography as if it were the worst imaginable use for good chemicals and photo paper. For three months he's photographed nothing in Florence but water and cobblestones. Today he follows Aïda as if she were leading him on a leash.

Aïda freezes, flattening herself against the house wall. It seems she's heard something, although there's still no one in the garden. After a moment she moves toward a bank of curtained French doors and tries a handle. The door opens, and she disappears inside. Joseph freezes. He waits until she beckons with her hand, then he slides in and closes the door behind him. They're gone. I am not about to go any farther. The sun is furious and the vines too low to provide any shelter. A bag containing lunch for four people hangs heavy on my back. I am the only one who has not brought any drawing tools. It was somehow understood that I would carry the food.

"We might as well wait here," Drew says. "Hopefully they'll be out soon."

"I hope." The bag slides off my shoulders and falls into the dust.

Drew reaches for the lunch. "I would have carried this for you," he says. His eyes rest for a moment on mine, but I know he is only trying to be polite.

There was a time when I was the one who got the attention, when my body was the one everyone admired. In junior high, where puberty was a kind of contest, you wanted to be the one with the tits out to here. I had my bra when I was nine, the first in our grade, which made me famous among my classmates. My mother, a busty lady herself, told me she was proud to see me growing up. I believed my breasts were a gift from God, and even let a few kids have an accidental rub at them. It wasn't until high school, when the novelty wore off and they grew to a D-cup, that I started to see things as they really were. Bathing suits did not fit right. I spilled out of the tops of sundresses. I looked ridiculous when running or jumping. Forget cheerleading. I began smashing those breasts down with sports bras, day and night.

It doesn't matter what the Baroque masters thought. The big breasts, the lush bodies, those are museum pieces now, and who cares if they stand for fertility and plenty, wealth and gluttony, or the fullest bloom of youth? Rubens's nudes made of cumulus clouds, Titian's milky, half-dressed beauties overflowing their garments, Lorenzo Lotto's big intelligent-eyed Madonnas—they have their place, and it is on a wall. No one remembers that a tiny breast meant desolation and deserts and famine.

Take Aïda on the billboard in Florence, wearing a gray Escada gown held up by two thin strands of rhinestones. Where the dress dips low at the side, there is a shadow like a closed and painted eyelid, just the edge of Aïda's tiny breast, selling this $6,000 dress. That is what you can do today with almost nothing.

The fact is, Aïda guessed right when she said I was a virgin. There were other girls at my high school, fat girls, who would go out by the train tracks at night and take off all their clothes. There were some who would give hand jobs. There were others who had sex for the first time when they were eleven. Few of these girls had dates for homecoming, and none of them held hands at school with the boys they met by the tracks at night. At the time, I would rather have died than be one of them.

But sometimes I think about how it might have been for those girls, who got to touch and be touched and to live with exciting varieties of shame. When I look at my drawings of men and women, there's a stiffness there, a glassiness I'm afraid comes from too little risk. It makes me dislike myself and perhaps it makes me a bad artist. Can these things be changed now that I am, in most ways, grown up? Is there a remedy for how I conducted my life all those years? Where do I begin?

Drew lies back on his elbows and whistles "Moon River." I wish I could relax. Somewhere below, my cousin stalks an artifact of her non-mother. I picture the tall, cool rooms with their crumbling ceilings and threadbare tapestries woven in dark colors. Maybe she will burn the place down. In another few months, I imagine, she will need to do something to get herself on the evening news. Being on a billboard can't be enough for her.

I put on Aïda's sun hat and tie its white ribbons beneath my chin. Just as I'm wondering if either of us will speak to the other all afternoon, Drew asks if I've decided to submit any works for display in the Del Reggio Gallery in Rome.

"*What* works?" I say. "You've seen my sliding people. Maybe I could do a little installation with a basket underneath each painting to catch the poor figure when she falls off the page."

"You have a talent, Mira. People criticize *my* work for being too realistic."

"But I don't plan to draw them expressionistically. They just come out that way. It's artistic stupidity, Drew, not talent."

"Well, then, I guess you'd better quit now," he says, shrugging. He picks up some fallen grapes, waxy and black, and throws them into the hammock of my skirt. "How about another profession? Sheepherding? Radio announcing? Hat design?"

"There's a fine idea." The words come out clipped and without humor. A dry silence settles between us, and I'm angry at myself for being nervous and at him for bringing up the exhibition. He knows his work will go into the show.

At times I think it would be terrible to have him touch me. I can imagine the disappointment he would show when I removed my dress. One hopes to find a painter who likes the old masters, like in the personal columns I've read in *The Chicago Tribune:* Lusty DWM w/taste for old wine and Rubens seeks SWF with full-bodied flavor. Would I ever dare to call?

"So what do you think of my little cousin?" I ask.

"Why?" he says. "What do you think of her?"

"She's had a hard past," I say, in an attempt at magnanimity. Because if I answered the question with honesty, I would blast Aïda to Turkmenistan. All our lives she has understood her advantage over me, and has exercised it at every turn. When I pass her billboard in town I can feel her gleeful disdain. No matter how well you paint, she seems to say, you will remain invisible next to me.

Perhaps because Drew is older I thought of him as enlightened in certain ways; but I saw how he looked at my cousin today with plain sexual appetite. I hand him a plum from our lunch bag and turn my face away from the sun because I am hot and tired and want to be far away from here.

As we eat, we hear the foreign-sounding *ee-oo* of an Italian police siren in the distance. Dread kindles in my chest. I imagine Aïda being wrested into handcuffs by a brown-shirted Italian policeman, and the shamefaced look she'll give Joseph as her lie comes crashing down. Will I be too sorry later to say I told her so? I can almost hear my mother's phone diatribe: *You let her break into a house with some boy? And just watched the police haul her off to an Italian jail*? Drew and I get to our feet. The house below is quiet and still. A boxy police car sweeps into the lane, dragging a billow of dust behind it. It roars down the hill and screeches to a stop somewhere in front of the house, where we can no longer see it. After a moment someone pounds on the front door.

Drew says, "We'd better go down."

"They'll see us."

"Suit yourself." He flicks the pit of his plum into the grapevines and starts down the hill.

I follow him toward the front of the house until we see the paved area where the car is parked. He is about to step onto the piazza. Panicked, I take his arm and pull him behind a stand of junipers at the side of the driveway. There are just enough bushes to hide both of us. The shadows are deep but there are places to look through the branches, and we can see the police officer who had been pounding on the front door. The other officer sits quietly in the car, engrossed in a map.

"This is ridiculous," Drew says. "We have to go in."

"No way," I whisper. "There's enough trouble already. What's the minimum penalty for breaking and entering in this country?"

Drew shakes his head. "Tell me I came to Florence to stand in a bush."

The front door opens slightly, and the policeman goes inside. After a few minutes the officer with the map gets out and goes to the door, then into the house. Everything is still. A bird I can't name alights near Drew's hand and bobs on a thin branch. We stand together in the dust. The heat coming off his body has an earthy smell like the beeswax soap nuns sell in the marketplace. If I extended my hand just a centimeter, I could touch his arm.

"Uh-oh," he says softly.

There are Aïda and Joseph being led from the house by the policemen. Aïda's hair is mussed as if there has been a struggle, and her dress hangs crooked at the shoulder. Joseph walks without looking at her. A woman in a black dress—a housekeeper from the looks of her—curses at them from the doorway. They're not in handcuffs, but the police aren't about to let them go, either. Just as the first policeman opens the car door, a chocolate-colored Mercedes appears at the top of the drive. The steel-haired housekeeper stiffens and points. "*La padrona di casa*," she says.

They hold Aïda and Joseph beside the police car, waiting for the Mercedes to descend into the piazza. When the car arrives and the dust clears, the lady of the house climbs out. She squares herself toward the scene in front of her villa. She is tall and lean. Her hair is caught in the kind of knot the Italian women wear, heavy and sweeping and low on the neck. Beneath her ivory jacket her shoulders are businesslike. She looks as if she would be more at home in New York or Rome than out here on this grape farm. She lowers her black sunglasses. With a flick of her hand toward Aïda and Joseph, she asks who the two criminals might be.

Aïda raises her chin and looks squarely at the woman. "*La vostra dottore*," she says. Your doctor.

The policemen roar with laughter.

The maid tells her padrona that Aïda was apprehended in the boudoir, trying on shoes. She had tried on nearly ten pairs before she was caught.

"You like my shoes?" the woman asks in English. She tilts her head, scrutinizing Aïda. "You look familiar to me."

"She's a model," Joseph says.

"Ah!" the woman says. "And you? You are a model too?" Her mouth is thin and agile.

"A photographer," Joe says.

"And you were trying on shoes also in my house?"

There is a silence. Joseph looks at Aïda for some clue as to what she wants him to say or do. Aïda looks around, and I almost feel as if she is looking for me, as if she thinks I might come out and save her now. Her eyes begin to dart between the padrona and the policemen, and her mouth opens. She lets her eyes flutter closed, then collapses against a policeman in an extremely realistic faint.

"Poor girl," the woman says. "Bring her into the house."

The police look disapproving, but they comply. One of them grabs her under the shoulders and the other takes her feet. Like an imperial procession they all enter the house, and the housekeeper closes the door behind them.

"She must be sick," Drew whispers. "Does she eat?"

"In a manner of speaking."

He climbs out of our hiding place and starts down toward the house. I have to follow him. I picture being home in bed, lying on my side and looking at the blank wall, a desert of comfort, no demands or disappointment. As I navigate the large stones at the edge of the piazza, my foot catches in a crevice and I lose my balance. There's a snap, and pain shoots through my left ankle. I come down hard onto my hip.

Drew turns around. "You okay?"

I nod, sideways, from the ground. He comes back to offer me his hand. It's torture getting up. My body feels as if it weighs a thousand pounds. When I test the hurt ankle, the pain makes my eyes water. I let go of Drew's hand and limp toward the door.

"Are you going to make it?" Drew asks.

"Sure," I say, but the truth is there's something awfully wrong. The pain tightens in a band around my lower leg. Drew rings the doorbell, and in a few moments the housekeeper opens the door. Her eyes are small and stern. She draws her gray brows together and looks at Drew. In his perfect Italian, he tells her that our friends are inside and that we would like to ask forgiveness of the lady of the house. She throws her hands heavenward and wonders aloud what will happen next. But she holds the door open and beckons us inside.

The entry hall is cool and dark like a wine cavern itself. There is a smell of fennel and coffee and dogs, and the characteristic dampness of Florentine architecture. Supporting myself against the stone wall, I creep along behind Drew, past tall canvases portraying the vintner's family, long-faced men and women arrayed in brocade and velvet and gold. The style is almost more Dutch than Italian, with angular light and deep reds and blues. In one portrait a seventeenth-century version of our padrona holds a lute dripping with flower garlands. She looks serene and pastoral, certainly capable of mercy. I take this for a good sign. We move past these paintings toward a large sunny room facing the back garden, whose

French doors I recognize as the ones Aïda slipped through not long ago. My cousin is stretched out on a yellow chaise longue with Joseph at her side. The policemen are nowhere to be seen. I imagine them drinking espresso in the kitchen with the inevitable cook. La Padrona sits next to Aïda with a glossy magazine open on her lap, exclaiming at what she sees. "Ah, yes, here you are again," she says. "God, what a gown." It's as though royalty has come for a visit. She seems reluctant to look away from the photographs when the maid enters and announces us as friends of the signorina.

"More friends?"

"Actually, Mira's my cousin," Aïda explains. "And that's Drew. He's another student."

Drew gives our padrona a polite nod. Then he goes to Aïda and crouches beside her chaise longue. "We saw you faint," he says. "Do you need some water?"

"She'll be fine," Joseph says, and gives him a narrow-eyed look.

Drew stands, raising his hands in front of him. "I asked her a simple question."

The padrona clears her throat. "Please make yourself comfortable," she says. "Maria will bring you a refreshment." She introduces herself as Pietà Cellini, the wife of the vintner. She says this proudly, although from the state of their house it seems the family wines haven't been doing so well in recent years. As she speaks she holds Aïda's hand in her own. "Isn't she remarkable, your cousin?" she asks. "So young."

"I'm awfully sorry about all this," I say. "We should be getting home."

"She's darling," says Signora Cellini. "My own daughter went to study in Rome two years ago. She's just a little older than Aïda. Mischievous, too."

"Is that so?" I say. The pain in my ankle has become almost funny. My head feels weightless and poorly attached.

"Aïda was just showing me her lovely pictures in *Elle*," our host says. "The poor girl had a shock just now, all those police. I'm afraid our housemaid was quite rude."

"I'm sure she was just protecting your house," I say.

Aïda sips water from a porcelain cup. Joseph takes it from her when she's finished and sets it down on a tiny gilt table. "Is that better?" he asks.

"You're so nice." Aïda pats his arm. "I'm sure it was just the heat."

Black flashes crowd the edges of my vision. The ankle has begun to throb. I look past them all, through the panes of the French doors and out into the garden, where an old man digs at a bed of spent roses. Dry-looking cuttings lie on the ground, and bees dive and hover around the man. He is singing a song whose words I cannot hear through the glass. I rest my forehead against my hand, wondering how I can stand to be here a moment longer. Aïda laughs, and Joseph's voice joins hers. It seems she has done this intentionally, in reparation for the thrown candlestick or the words I said to her, or even because all my life I have had a mother and she has had none. What a brilliant success I would be if I could paint the scene in this sunny room, glorious Aïda in careful disarray, the two men repelled by one another and drawn to her, the elegant woman leaning over her with a porcelain cup. Sell it. Retire to Aruba. I can already feel the paint between my fingers, under my nails, sliding beneath my fingertips on the canvas. And then I hear the padrona's voice coming from what seems a great distance, calling not Aïda's name but my own. "Mira," she says, "Good God. What happened to your ankle?"

In defiance of all my better instincts, I look down. At first it seems I am looking at a foreign object, some huge red-and-purple swelling where my ankle used to be. It strains against the straps of my sandal as if threatening to burst. "I got hurt," I say, blinking against a contracting darkness, and then there is silent nothing.

It is nighttime. I do not recall getting back to the apartment, nor do I remember undressing or getting into bed. The room is quiet. There is a bag of crushed ice on my ankle, and an angel bending over it as if it had already died. Translucent wings rise from the angel's back, and its face is inclined over my foot. Its hair shines blue in the moonlight. It murmurs an incomprehensible prayer.

The mosquito netting fills with wind and then hangs limp again, brushing Aïda's shoulders. Her face is full of concentration. She touches the swollen arch of my foot. I can hardly feel it. You could help me if you wanted to, she might say now. You have lived longer than I have and could let me know how it is, but you don't. You let me dance and giggle and look like an idiot. You like it. You wish it. Is she saying this?

"How did we get home?" I ask her. My voice sounds full of sleep.

"You're awake," she says. "You sure messed up your ankle."

"It feels like there are bricks on my chest."

"Signora Cellini gave you Tylenol with codeine. It knocked you out."

Sweet drug. My wisdom-tooth friend. One should have it around. "Where are the guys?"

"Home. We made quite a spectacle."

"You did."

"That's what I do, Cousin Mira."

"*I* don't."

"Was I the only one to faint today?" She raises her eyebrows at me.

"Well, I didn't do it on purpose."

"You'll have to go to a doctor tomorrow."

"So be it. This is your fault, you know," I tell her. I mean for it to be severe, but the last part comes out *falyuno*. I am almost asleep again and grateful for that. With my eyelids half-closed I can see the wings rising from her shoulders again, and her feet might be fused into one, and who knows, she might after all be sexless and uninvolved with the commerce of this world, and I might be the Virgin Mary, receiving the impossible news.

The next morning Aïda calls a cab and we go down to the university infirmary, where an American nurse named Betsy feels my ankle and shakes her head. "X-ray," she says, her blond ponytail swinging back and forth. "This looks ugly." My ankle, if I were to reproduce it on a canvas, would require plenty of aquamarine and ocher and Russian red. The doctor handles me gently. He tells the technician to take plenty of pictures. In another room the doctor puts my films up on a lighted board. He shows me a hairline fracture, which looks to me like a tiny mountain range etched into my bone. He does not understand why I smile when he gives me the bad news. How can I explain to him how apt it is? Drew would recommend a self-portrait.

When I return to the waiting room wearing a fiberglass cast from toes to mid-calf, I find Aïda holding a croissant on a napkin. I feel as if I will faint from hunger.

"Hi, gimp," she says. There's a smirk. I'd like to whack her with my new weapons. Instead we head for the door and walk down Via Rinaldi toward a trattoria where I can find some breakfast. The sun is out, and the *zanzare*. Big, fat ones. Unlike American mosquitoes, these actually hurt when they bite. It's the huge proboscis. At least my ankle is safe from that for a while.

The doctor has prescribed normal activity, with caution until I learn to use the crutches better. It's my first time on them—I always wanted them when I was a kid, but somehow managed to escape injury—and I think I will stay home as long as possible. Time to paint. No more vineyards. Aïda can do what she likes for the last two days of her visit.

At the trattoria we have a marble-topped table on the sidewalk, and a kind waiter looks at me with pity. He brings things we do not order, a little plate of biscotti and tiny ramekins of flavored butter for our *pane*. Aïda twirls her hair and looks at her feet. She is quiet today and has neglected to put on the customary makeup: something to make her lips shine, a thin dark line around the eyes, a pink stain on the cheeks. She looks almost plain, like anyone else's cousin. She actually eats the free biscotti.

Our waiter sets espresso cups on the table. Aïda's growth will be stunted forever by the staggering amount of caffeine she has consumed in Florence. Of course, her father doesn't allow it back home. "Does it hurt?" she asks, pointing to the ankle.

"Not so much anymore," I say. "All that good pain medicine."

"Too bad about the cast. I really mean it. They itch something awful."

Great.

"Now, can I ask you one question, Aïda?" I say.

"One." She lifts her cup and grins at her sneakers.

"What was all that malarkey about your mother? I mean, for God's sake."

There's a long silence. Her lips move slightly as if she's about to answer, but no words come. She sets the cup down and begins to twist her hands, thin bags of bones, against each other. The knuckles crack. "*I* don't know," she says finally. "It was just something to say."

"A little ridiculous, don't you think? Making Joseph break into the house with you?"

"I didn't make anyone do anything." She frowns. "He could have stayed behind with you."

"You sorcered him, Aïda. You knew you were doing it."

Aïda picks up her tiny spoon and stirs the espresso, her eyes becoming serious and downcast. "I did look up my actual mother once," she says.

The admission startles me. I sit up in the iron chair. "When?"

"Last year. After the accident. I imagined dying without ever knowing her, and that was too scary. I didn't tell my dad about it, because you know, he wants me to see him as *both* parents."

"But how did you find her?"

"There was a government agency. France has tons of them, they're so socialized. A man helped me locate a file, and there she was, I mean her name and information about her.

Her parents' address in Rouen. My grandparents, can you believe it?"

I imagine a white-haired lady somewhere on an apple farm, wondering to whom the high, clear voice on the phone could belong. It sounds like the voice of a ghost, a child she had who died when she was twelve. She answers the girl's questions with fear in her chest. Does a phone call from a spirit mean that one is close to death?

"They gave me her phone number and address. She was living in Aix-en-Provence. I took a bus there and stood outside her apartment building for hours, and when it rained I stood in someone's vestibule. I didn't even know which window was hers. It's just as well, I guess. She wouldn't have wanted to see me anyhow."

I don't want to believe this story. It seems designed to make me pity her. Yet there's an embarrassment in her face that suddenly makes her look very young, like a child who has admitted to a misdeed. "Are you going to try again?" I ask.

"Maybe sometime," she says. "Maybe after my career."

"That might be a long time," I say.

"Probably not," she says, her eyes set on something in the distance. "I'll have a few good years, and I'd better make enough money to retire on. I don't know what other job I could do."

I consider this. "So what will you do with yourself afterward?"

"I don't know. Go to Morocco with my father. Have kids. Whatever people do."

I think of those pictures of my uncle in couture evening gowns, his skin milky, his waist slender as a girl's. His graceful fingers hold roses or railings or *billets-doux*. His hair hangs long and thick, a shiny mass down his back. He now wears turtlenecks and horn-rimmed glasses; there are veins on the backs of his hands, and his beautiful hair is gone. I wonder how this can happen to Aïda. She seems eternal, the exception to a rule. Can she really be mortal? Even when she fell off the bridge and chanted fever-songs, I knew she would survive to see international fame. In the glossy pages of Signora Cellini's magazines and those of women all over the world, she will never, never change.

But here on the sidewalk at the trattoria she bites a hangnail, and looks again at my foot. "We should get you home," she says. "You need some rest." I wonder if she will survive what will happen to her. I wonder if she will live to meet her mother. There are many things I would ask her if only we liked each other better.

One afternoon, perhaps a month after Aïda's return to Paris, I buy a bottle of inexpensive Chianti and a round loaf of bread and head down to the ancient marketplace by the Arno. There, in the shadow of a high colonnade, the tall bronze statue of Il Porcelino guards the empty butcher stalls. It's easy to move around on the crutches now, although the cobbled streets provide a challenge. I wear long loose dresses to hide my cast.

At the center of the piazza the white-robed Moroccans have spread their silver and leather goods on immaculate sheets. They sing prices as I pass. Because I have some *lire* in my pocket, I buy a thin braided bracelet of leather. Perhaps I will send it to my cousin. Perhaps I will keep it for myself. Down by the river, pigeons alight on the stones and groom their feathers. I sit with my legs dangling over a stone ledge and uncork my round-bellied bottle, and the wine tastes soft and woody. It's bottled by the Cellinis. It's pretty good, certainly not bad enough to make them go broke. I drink to their health and to the health of people everywhere, in celebration of a rather bizarre occurrence. Two days ago I sold a painting. The man who bought it laughed aloud when I said he had made a bad choice. He is an opera patron and food critic from New York City, the godson of my painting professor back in the States. He attended our winter exhibition last January, and happened to be visiting Rome when the Del Reggio Gallery was showing our work.

It is not a painting of Aïda dancing in the grapevines, her hair full of leaves. It is not an unapologetic self-portrait, nor a glowing Tuscan landscape. It is a large sky-blue square canvas with two Chagall-style seraphim in the foreground, holding a house and a tree and a child in their cupped hands. It is called *Above the Farm*. In slightly darker blue, down below, you can make out the shadow of a tornado. Why he bought this painting, I do not know. But there's one thing I can tell you: those angels have no feet.

Although it's interesting to think of my painting hanging in this man's soaring loft in Manhattan, it makes me sad to think I will never see it again. I always feel comforted, somehow, looking at that child standing by his house and tree, calm and resigned to residence in the air. Five hundred feet off the ground, he's still the same boy he was when he stood on the earth. I imagine myself sitting on this ledge with Aïda, when she is old and I am famous. She will look at me as if I take up too much space, and I will want to push her into the Arno. But perhaps by then we will love ourselves less fiercely. Perhaps the edges of our mutual hate will have worn away, and we will have already said the things that need to be said.

William Wadsworth

Galaxies

for Samuel Wadsworth

I

A yacht at night strung with lights on the black
tide rolls to the rhythm of a trio playing
"Waltz for Debbie." The Milky Way looks on
as Mr. Lucky in his white suit strolls the deck
   whistling the theme, keeping watch on the 1950s

from just offshore, his look cool as light
from an extinguished star still seeking its faraway
destination, while the piano inside,
the highballs of laughter, the ice against
   the glass, chime together, and the black waves

and the white hull with its portholes tunneling into
hidden worlds describe a universe
that pre-existed you. This vision of perfect
autonomy, this private eye, patrols
   the night on a flickering screen, adrift in the 1950s.

II

Your hunger for milk was enormous, filling entire
nights in your mother's arms. But at first you wouldn't
nurse, as though you had to learn the knack
to suck. Such gravity to your small gaze,
   pondering—how could it be that a labor of love

must follow a state of grace? So the night nurse—
one Mary Muldoon on the midnight shift—whistled
to catch your eye, and coaxed your lips to seek
   the one who so tenderly docked you to this galaxy.

And then you gave that look, the attentive look
with one lifted brow that still draws the world
so easily around you. And the light which in waves
washes a white basin of stars poured
in your eyes the milky vision of your mother's
   body arching over yours, haloed in bliss.

III

So it seemed from the start that you were hungry for light
knowing the world would grow brighter with you.
The luna moth hurtling tonight against
my screen may be the harbinger of your
   desire. But I can't help believing it was not light

but light intensified by the love of light
that led a poet in the end to invoke
the asphodel, to say that love which begins
in a chase through darkness always closes in
   a thunderstroke of light. So now your autonomy

begins, and I consider your voyage out
and the long passages of solitude
under one star or another that will test
a man of such luck and appetite. But remain
   attentive, and listen: the stars are whistling your theme.

Two Poems by John Reibetanz

From Chedworth Roman Villa, Many Happy Returns

Dear Uncle Chris, welcome back to my mind
  after so many years. Forgive me for
    not thinking you up sooner: the coiled-vine

repeats on these unearthed mosaic floors
  should have been all you needed to slip through
    oblivion, the way a live vine's flowers

escape from undergrowth. Three shades of blue
  spun the same triple braid in small square tiles
    winding over the kitchen table where you

inlaid blue-petalled limestone flowers—a child's
  dream garden, planted with such solid faith
    this child's muscles couldn't move it an inch.

We roamed it after meals. You taught me the braid's
  name among tilesetters, *guilloche*, your tongue
    loving the sounds as it still loved the brandy

that drove Aunt Helen away before I was born,
  and left you thirsting after summer guests
    for your big house by the water at Cold Spring.

•

Today, it took the eyes of Spring herself
  in warm brown tile to summon you. She ran
    naked towards me, silk scarf beneath her breasts

floating outstretched before her like a ribbon
  at a race she was about to win, only
    the thin glaze holding her back in Roman Britain.

Her eyes escaped, artlessly breaking free—
  the tiles a "simple provincial product" too
    big for her head. Their emptiness pulled me

back to the first time I had ever seen you
  without your bottle-glass-thick lenses, put
    away for safety by the nurse. Brown pools

deep enough to drown in—you had tried it,
  giving up quick swigs for the long, unbroken
    indraft of madness—emptied by shock treatments,

every glimmer of recognition gone.
  Your eyes' light would return; your trembling hands
    could never weave those tile ribbons again.

•

The ribbons only seem to pass under
  each other and come up again: *guilloche*,
    the "universal repeat," is not three bands

spiralling in one long embrace. Our wish
  for endlessness spins endless rounds of thread
    from isolated sets of flat square chips.

Our longing eyes soften the tile's knife-edge
  to curve: they warm stone out of torpor, couple
    separateness, and bring life to the dead

mineral, the lost woman, the loved uncle.
  It is our thirst that sets these waters flowing,
    dream-blue and body-warm, undrinkable:

unlike the waters running from the spring
   you showed me once, that gave your town its name.
      We knelt over a gap between stones, filling

empty milk bottles with a leaping gleam.
   Held up, it looked like nothing; but my tongue,
      tasting, met fangs that bit deep, and went numb.

The Finger Puppets in the Attic Dollhouse

If they, more petite
   than the mice whose flittings
      have pillaged their robes' sparkled trim,

stood tiptoe
   on the plumped felt tops
      of their thimble-sized footstools

to scrutinize
   the worn fabric
      of this room's blue distances,

would they locate
   the source of lightning bolts
      in our faces' wrinkled pleats

and construe the stars'
   dance from the tattered
      embroidery of our steps,

or find in our seamless
   unraveling years
      the tissue of apocalypse?

Two Poems by Joan Murray

Possession

MacDowell Colony

A deer!—nibbling on the few green things
that grow in my strawy meadow.
Mine, we say here: *my* studio, *my* meadow, *my* road.
It is as it is. We were born
to possess it all and more. There's no longer
a chance to change direction. So have one. *Have* a meadow.
Try it on—there are black-eyed Susans in your hair.
Have a deer. Have a deer fly—(I had *two*
of them yesterday. My stained tablet backs me up).
Have a swallow. Try to hold it in your throat
as it goes down beyond the pines of your forest.
But first feel its presence, try to catch
its essence. Before the words intrude.

Or were they there before you even *saw* it?
My. *Mine*. The exultant mind!—
as incapable as an ant of evading the trail
to its hole. But look down into that hole:
it's full of everything you've seen or can hope to see.
Do you think you could, for once,
see something—maybe a deer—and not *think* the word?
Even if you tried with all your "faculties,"
even if you tricked yourself that you had,
some part of your mind would have whispered *deer*
(the mind's equivalent of saying *mine*).

Now you *possess* it. It is *your* deer.
See how nicely it fits with all the other things:
it finds the stall of its category—the strawy room

in your father's house that was prepared for it.
Wasn't that you at the door with your mother
as she pointed to the things: *meadow*, *swallow*, *deer*,
so you would know them when you woke?
The things she overlooked, you discovered
in your books. You showed them to your mind,
and now when you see something rise from the meadow
with its gold furred shape tapering into a sting,
your mind rushes in, pointing to the page:
Honeybee, it tells you. (*My* honeybee.)

Why would you want to stop it now? Didn't you
reward it with gold stars till now it struts like a priest,
mediating all your experience through its psalter?
What are *you*? you ask it.
It sifts the gilt-edged pages of itself, it moves
the satin ribbon to a field of gray—densely coiled
—through which hum the resplendent neurons—
extending themselves, synapse to synapse.
In the pots on their darting hips
is everything you've ever thought or known.
I am your *mind*, it says. *My* mind, it says,
as it contemplates itself—as if it had
created itself—with vanity and humility.

Looking for the Parade

for Tony Phillips, Memorial Day

I

The women from Yaddo's kitchen
told us there'd be a parade.
(Ever since they were children—long before
their parents were children!—there had been

a parade.) We didn't ask where it would go,
knowing it would have to go down
whichever street lies along the backbone of the town
—and here in Saratoga is called Broadway.
And it would march from wherever the gentry live
to whatever park holds the cannon,
scrapped from whichever war—
like this one on Union Avenue,
where this morning, spike-haired punks are sleeping,
and a bride is yawning, and a pair of twins,
one blue-, the other, brown-eyed,
are improvising a ceremony at the side of their stroller.

And we were certain the whole town
would be waiting on this grass
where the tamed mallards poke for crumbs—
and a pair of gray-haired lovers touch
with such slow tenderness—that we smile at their progress
—till they suddenly grow self-conscious.
And at that moment, a whistle in the distance
would dispatch a coterie of drums and brass
from a boys' club. Then, a drill team,
filled out with decoy guns and banners.
A squad of twirlers and cadets.
A company, fatigued and slightly out of breath
from Vietnam. A women's auxiliary,
uniformly overweight, but stepping lightly.
—And bringing up the rear, a white-haired man,
pushed by (one last time) in his rolling silver chair.

And we would stand among the people of this town,
waiting for that parade to come
—our heads inclined in the same direction—
to catch the first uncertain notes
or glimpse a flash of colors
between the bobbing heads and shoulders,
that line their route down Broadway.

And despite our belief that we could keep our distance,
some clumsy salute or off-key rallying strain
might touch us as we listen—
might quicken our pulses as we wait in formation,
pressed shoulder to shoulder.
Then we'd have to struggle for a moment,
blink our eyes, force ourselves to smile,
and whisper to each other how corny it all is—
with wave after wave of passing American life.

II

Still looking for the parade, we drive up Broadway—
hearing, blow by blow, what will happen
When Johnny Comes Marching Home on the FM radio.
The melody is gloomy—despite the lyric's try
for a jaunty encouragement.
They must have known, even then, in our internecine war—
after the unfulfilled waiting, the contradictory news
and the unexplained silence
that permits a general, willful delusion,
that there might be no parade.
Even today, there are no *men cheering*,
no *boys shouting*.
The *ladies—they* have not *turned out*
—not even the women from the kitchen.
There's still no sign of a parade.
Though we've kept on looking for what seems a century.

I point with hope to a corner
where a man with a rolling cart—
hung with T-shirts and Caribbean art—
is arranging his display as if preparing for a crowd
—(But Tony's sure there was a cart there all last week).
We spot a family turning onto Broadway
with caps and visors, binoculars and cameras.
But they're too well-dressed—

they've got no folding chairs or cooler chests
—(Only tourists from another city).
And what of those three girls on that bench,
tanned and leggy and a little giggly?
They scan us as we pass—then go back to eating lunch—
without a sign of disillusionment
—(knowing that in time,
someone better will come by and pick them up).

But then at a light—a man in a tie-dyed shirt,
middle-aged and thick in the waist,
calls to us from the curb, "What time is the parade?"
He's been looking up Broadway,
he's been waiting for Johnny.
He wants to give him that *hearty welcome*—
—It's a new age now—we all want to *feel gay*.
We've put aside our revolutions—our radical opinions
—Even our campus insurrections are fading into history.
It's time to walk with Johnny to the park
and stand beside him (through the long-
winded speeches, filled with peaceful lies).
It's time to shake his hand—
and go and spread the news: that Johnny's
come marching home, and his legs still work
—and maybe all of that was worth it.

III

A policeman says, "There's no parade
on Broadway. You should get yourselves
to the Battlefield—and see if *one's* out there."
The bridge across the lake is closed.
We've got no map but turn to the south
down a rubble road, lined with toppling walls
that keep someone's weedy field
from invading someone else's.
Finally a sign says "Burgoyne Road"

—so we *know* we're getting close:
we both remember Johnny Burgoyne—from
our grade-school history.
Now we follow his road—till the arrows
show us where to find: "The Gift Shop,"
"The Picnic Grounds," and "The Battlefield Parking Lot."
But there's no parade today—"just the permanent exhibit."

In case after case, the little men stand watch.
March on their little paths.
Fire their tiny muskets.
And fall to their tiny deaths.
But above them on the walls, huge painted figures—
more harrowing than Goya's—glower from the dark.
But the terror's not intentional
—It's only "art"—meant to be "inspirational."
Look at the case with Morgan's Rangers after the opening
  volley:
they were young and green and might have run or given up,
but they rallied and won,
and now they're savoring victory,
resting on scattered stumps,
living hour to hour—and spared the dramatic irony
that we (made privy to their history) are forced to consider:
that they'll *all* be dead tomorrow.

But it's yesterday's war—
just a clumsy reconstruction,
made of bits of colored paper and interactive buttons.
Look at the thousands of painted leaves
—cut and pasted, one by one, on a dozen twiggy trees.
And listen to that stentorian text
—with its sound effects and Hessian accents,
rising from a case, that's supposed to show a place
just down the road—where (if it were *only*
the first week of September—as we're told),
the leaves would *never* have turned brown.

Probably *all* of it's revisionist
—and in any case, it's got *nothing* to do with us.
But then, in the next case, is a powder belt (hardly even used)—
and a collar and an officer's glove—that were dug up
in a field—with a pair of someone's boots.

IV

It's already after three, when we get our lunch pails from the car
and follow the arrows to "The Picnic Grounds."
But all the tables have been claimed by families
(who've laid down their checkered cloths
and turned up their radios—to delineate their boundaries).
We drive on to Victory. But there's no safe place
on the cliff above the millrace at the ruined Victory Mills.
And across the creek where the slope's less steep,
there's a spill of unsettling debris,
left by some drifter before the winter.
We read the scraps of last year's news—
and wonder at the unopened cans of beans
(in his cache of unredeemed bottles).
And marvel at how the weeds
have flowered in the armpits of his sleeves—
and in the crotch of his faded trousers.

We head north again, looking for some simple
patch of grass: uncrowded, uncluttered—fairly level.
And there (like an answer to a child's eavesdropped prayer)
is the stately Schuyler Mansion, with a tour bus parked in back
—and in front, its *sprawling lawn*.
We pick a spot near the fence—
as far from the entrance as it's possible to get.
But someone cracks the door—to extend a pointing hand—
and warn us that we're trespassing.
We turn west this time through Schuylerville

—to the one thing we can find without a map:
the Battlefield Monument—a towering Gothic obelisk—
the tallest structure of its kind,
a turn-of-the-century hallowed shrine
—though it wasn't built where the battle was fought,
but as a marketing device for a sleepy village cemetery.

We climb the hill between the rows of markers
—past the large ones—with their uneroded boasts,
and the mid-sized ones—aggrieved at the intrusion
in what they'd counted on would be their middle years.
And, tucked in among them, the small, nameless infants
—who've contentedly *inherited the earth*.
I settle on the grave of Lydia Mott, a woman my own age,
who settled here a hundred years ago.
She's got a mid-sized stone, a little shade,
and only a few mosquitoes.
From her plot, there's a fine view of Vermont,
the lower Adirondacks—and the distant field in Stillwater
—where the battle was really fought.
But what does it matter? Lydia Mott doesn't care
what happened—or where—Or if there's no parade.
Or who's come to eat their lunch.

V

Relaxed on our graves,
we raise the tagged lids of our lunch pails,
and, noticing our names, we joke about how well
they make us fit among our company.
Only two cars pass us in an hour,
and then there's a rumbling down below
—and up between the markers, rolls a pack of bikers,
(ignoring all the set-in-stone requests for "rest" and "peace").
There are ten—with a grizzly bearded leader at the head—
fitted out in all his militant regalia:
the red and blue tattoos, the gleaming metal-studded cuffs

—and the vest that only skims his fleshy torso.
He stops his bike twenty feet from us
and stares our way, considering his plans.
The rest fan out behind him,
fidgety—in the sun, their chains and leather.

Their motors turning over,
two forward ones begin a drill maneuver:
making narrow turns
on the graves that say "Infant" and "Mother."
Though we can't begin to comprehend its meaning—
or predict where their pageantry is leading—
it's clear who's signaling the moves (he grimaces occasionally,
so I can see that most of his lower teeth are gone).
When at last he's ready, he raises his right hand,
and his right-hand man—pulls up till he's nearly at our feet,
and without dismounting or shutting off his engine,
he leans and asks: "Where's the parade?"
As they rumble back down, with undaunted bluster,
we smile at each other—
glad to be left with the safe, quiet dead
in the clouds of settling dust.

But we've got no plans to stay with them *forever*—
pressed shoulder to shoulder in their regimented rows—
in the kind of place our new age doesn't bother with at all.
But the grass still grows here,
and someone comes and mows—and leaves a whistle in the air
to move among the immovable formation:
the long parade going nowhere.
No, you'll never find *us* here!
—We might be scattered in a stream—or under a favorite
tree—
fooling ourselves
that we've escaped the *ultimate* conformity.

But despite our hopes to avoid its trappings,
or at least be able to explain
that *we* were different—that we liked to joke—and never
took things too seriously, we'll take our places, just as they did
—and find it just as easy.

Matthew Greenfield

At the Goethe Institut

Berlin, August 1992

Is there a secret map of the lives of men
In the slow drift of stars and clouds of stars?
Can I build a house out of hydrogen
Or trace the figures of my ancestors,
Remote and perfect, in those tentative
Conjunctions? Will they teach me how to live?

That nebula has the shape of a book,
Perhaps one owned by those cousins, the Cohens.
With the paper turned to ash and the ink to smoke
The clean and trembling words could have risen
Translated out of their mortal language
Into a luminous and final knowledge.

Would they know Greek? *Memory* has a root
That is the name of a goddess, the mother of poetry
And her sister, the one who plays her flute
Softly, and will not speak. An elegy
Could start with them, with the sweetness of names
In catalogs, and offerings, and funeral games.

O what an endlesse worke, an old song says,
To count the sea's abundant progeny,
So huge their numbers, and so numberless
Their nation. That was a joyful ceremony,
That marriage of the rivers, but the guests
Have all gone home, and the sun has set in the west.

O what an endlesse worke. Lotte Cohen.
To count the starres on hye. Mitze. Meyer Cohen.

delinearam manobras de protecção, mas os vagares da História e as rudimentares técnicas de comunicação no passado retardaram a alongaram os processos de envolvimento, absorção e substituição, o que nos permitia, sem maiores inquietações, considerar que tudo isto era da ordem do natural e do lógico, como se na torre de Babel tivesse ficado decidido o destino de cada língua: vida, paixão e morte, triunfo e derrota, ressurreição nunca.

«Ora, as línguas, hoje, batem-se. Não há declarações de guerra, mas a luta é sem quartel. A História, que antes não fazia mais do que andar, voa agora, e os actuais meios de comunicação de massa excedem, na sua manifestação mais simples, toda a capacidade imaginativa daqueles que, como o autor destas linhas, fazem da imaginação, precisamente, instrumento de trabalho. Claro que desta guerra de falantes e escreventes não se esperam, apesar de tudo, resultados definitivos em curto prazo. A inércia das línguas é um factor, também ele, de retardamento, mas as consequências derradeiras, verificáveis não sei quando, mas previsíveis, mostrarão, então demasiado tarde, que o emurchecimento prematuro da mais alta folha daquela árvore prenunciava já a extinção de toda a floresta.

«Línguas que hoje ainda apenas se apresentam como hegemónicas em superfície tendem a penetrar nos tecidos profundos das línguas subalternizadas, sobretudo se estas não souberam encontrar em si mesmas uma energia vital e cultural que lhes permitisse oporem-se ao desbarato a que se vêem sujeitas, agora que as comunicações no nosso planeta são o que são. Hoje, uma língua que não se defende, morre. Não de morte súbita, já o sabemos, mas irá caindo aos poucos num estado de consumpção que poderá levar séculos a consumar-se, dando em cada momento a ilusão de que continua vivaz, e por esta maneira afagando a indolência ou mas-

A galley page from Cadernos de Lanzarote (Lanzarote Diaries).

© J. Frade, 1997

José Saramago

The Art of Fiction CLV

On October 8, 1998, after several years on the unofficial short list, José Saramago was awarded the Nobel Prize for Literature—the first Portuguese writer to be so decorated. Asked his thoughts on receiving the prize, he said, "I will not take on the duties of the Nobel as would the winner of the beauty contest, who has to be shown off everywhere . . . I don't aspire to that kind of throne, nor could I, of course."

José Saramago was born in 1922 to a family of rural workers of modest means from the central Ribatejo section of Portugal. When he was two years old, the family moved to Lisbon, where his father worked as a policeman. In his teenage years, economic hardships made it necessary for Saramago to transfer from a regular high school to a vocational school—he would later work at a variety of jobs, including as a mechanic, before turning to writing full time.

In 1947, at age twenty-four, Saramago published his first novel, Land of Sin (Terra do Pecado). *Originally titled* The Widow, *it was renamed by the publisher in the hope that the racier title would sell more copies. (Saramago later commented that at that age he knew nothing of widows or sin.) He did not publish again for nineteen years. In 1966 his first collection of poems,* The Possible Poems (Os Poemas Possíveis), *appeared; and in 1977 he published a second novel,* Manual of Painting and Calligraphy. *During the sixties and seventies Saramago also was active in journalism, working as assistant director of* Díario de Notícias *for a short time; during particularly lean times, he supported himself by translating from the French. In 1969 he joined the Portuguese Communist Party, of which he has remained a committed member—his writing is linked intricately to social commentary and politics.*

With the publication of Raised Up from the Ground (Levantado do Chão) *in 1980, written in the wake of the 1974 Carnation Revolution, Saramago at last established his voice as a novelist. The story of three generations of agricultural laborers from the Alentejo region of Portugal, it received wide attention as well as the City of Lisbon Prize. The publication of* Baltasar and Blimunda *in 1982 catapulted his career internationally—in 1987 it became his first novel to appear in the United States. His next novel,* The Year of the Death of Ricardo Reis, *received the Portuguese PEN Club Prize and Britain's coveted Independent Foreign Fiction Award. His success continued with* The Stone Raft, *a fantastical criticism of Europe's struggle to assert its Europeanness, in which the Iberian Peninsula breaks apart from Europe and sails down the Atlantic Ocean in search of its Latin American and African roots. In 1989* The History of the Siege of Lisbon *appeared. Saramago acknowledged in a recent article that there is a lot of him in the protagonist of that novel, Raimundo Silva, a middle-aged, isolated proofreader who falls in love with his boss, an attractive, younger editor who saves him from emotional mediocrity. The novel is dedicated to his wife (as are all his subsequent books), the Spanish journalist Pilar del Rio, whom he married in 1988.*

In 1991 Saramago published The Gospel According to Jesus Christ, *which received the Portuguese Writers' Association Prize and a nomination for the European Union literary contest Ariosto. However, the Portuguese government, bowing to its conservative elements and pressure from the Catholic Church, banned the book from the competition. "It was totally unjustified," Saramago complained, "for something of this nature to have occurred with democracy fully in place in Portugal. Is there any government that can justify such a barbaric act? It was very painful for me."*

Soon after the controversy, Saramago and his wife left Lisbon, where he had lived for most of his life, and moved to the island of Lanzarote in the Spanish Canary Islands, where they still live with their three dogs—a terrier and two medium-sized poodles, Camões, Pepe and Greta—in a house they built next door to his sister-in-law. Since moving there Saramago has published two novels: Blindness, *a chilling parable of modern man's folly and his ability to inflict harm on his fellow man, and* All the Names (Todos os Nomes)*; as well as five volumes of his* Lanzarote Diaries (Cadernos de Lanzarote).

The interview took place on a sunny afternoon in March, 1997, at his home in Lanzarote. (He was in the process of becoming an adoptive son of the island.) His wife gave a quick tour of the house, including his study: a rectangular and orderly room lined with books, a desk with his computer, which he pronounced "an excellent machine," in the center. A larger office—with a wall of windows providing a view of Puerto del Carmen, the nearby island of Fuertaventura, the *beach and the metallic blue sky of Lanzarote—was being built on the second floor. Occasionally interrupted by the sounds of construction and the barking dogs, who dragged Pilar around entangled in their leashes, the conversation was marked most by Saramago's sharp sense of humor as well as his efforts to put his guest at ease—*minha querida *(my dear), he often reassured me as we talked.*

INTERVIEWER

Do you miss Lisbon?

JOSÉ SARAMAGO

It is not exactly missing or not missing Lisbon. If indeed missing, as the poet said, is that sentiment—that chilling of the spine—then the truth is that I do not feel that chilling of the spine.

I do think about it. We have many friends there and we go there once in a while, but the sensation I have in Lisbon now is that I don't know where to go anymore—I don't know how to *be* in Lisbon anymore. When I am there for a few days, or for a week or two, of course I go back to my old habits. But I am always thinking about coming back here as soon as possible. I like this place and the people here. I live well here. I don't think I will ever leave. Well, I will, after all we all have to leave one day, but I will only go against my will.

INTERVIEWER

When you moved to Lanzarote, away from the surroundings in which you had lived and written for so many years, did you accustom yourself immediately to this space, or did you miss your previous work space?

SARAMAGO

I adapted easily. I believe myself to be the type of person who does not complicate his life. I have always lived my life without dramatizing things, whether the good things that have happened to me or the bad. I simply live those moments.

Of course, if I feel sorrow, I feel it, but I do not . . . Let me say it another way: I do not look for ways of being interesting.

I am now writing a book. It would be much more interesting for me to tell you the torture I endure, the difficulty in constructing the characters, the nuances of the complicated narrative. What I mean is that I do what I have to do as naturally as possible. For me, writing is a job. I do not separate the work from the act of writing like two things that have nothing to do with each other. I arrange words one after another, or one in front of another, to tell a story, to say something that I consider important or useful, or at least important or useful to me. It is nothing more than this. I consider this my job.

INTERVIEWER

How do you work? Do you write every day?

SARAMAGO

When I am occupied with a work that requires continuity, a novel, for example, I write every day. Of course, I am subjected to all kinds of interruptions at home and interruptions due to traveling, but other than that, I am very regular. I am very disciplined. I do not force myself to work a certain number of hours per day, but I do require a certain amount of written work per day, which usually corresponds to two pages. This morning I wrote two pages of a new novel, and tomorrow I shall write another two. You might think two pages per day is not very much, but there are other things I must do—writing other texts, responding to letters; on the other hand, two pages per day adds up to almost eight hundred per year.

In the end, I am quite normal. I don't have odd habits. I don't dramatize. Above all, I do not romanticize the act of writing. I don't talk about the anguish I suffer in creating. I do not have a fear of the blank page, writer's block, all those things that we hear about writers. I don't have any of those problems, but I do have problems just like any other person doing any other type of work. Sometimes things do not come out as I want them to, or they don't come out at all. When things do not come out as well as I would have liked, I have to resign myself to accepting them as they are.

INTERVIEWER

Do you compose directly on a computer?

SARAMAGO

Yes, I do. The last book I wrote on a classic typewriter was *The History of the Siege of Lisbon*. The truth is, I had no difficulty in adapting to the keyboard at all. Contrary to what is often said about the computer compromising one's style, I don't think it compromises anything, and much less if it is used as I use it—like a typewriter. What I do on the computer is exactly what I would do on the typewriter if I still had it, the only difference being that it is cleaner, more comfortable and faster. Everything is better. The computer has no ill effects on my writing. That would be like saying that switching from writing by hand to writing on a typewriter would also cause a change in style. I don't believe that to be the case. If a person has his own style, his own vocabulary, how can working on a computer come to alter those things?

However, I do continue to have a strong connection—and it is natural that I should—to paper, to the printed page. I always print each page that I finish. Without the printed page there I feel . . .

INTERVIEWER

You need tangible proof.

SARAMAGO

Yes, that's it.

INTERVIEWER

After you have finished those two pages per day, do you then make alterations to your text?

SARAMAGO

Once I have reached the end of a work, I reread the whole text. Normally at that point there are some alterations—small changes relating to specific details or style, or changes to make the text more exact—but never major ones. About ninety percent of my work is in the first writing I put down, and that stays as is. I do not do what some writers do—that is, to write a twenty-page abstract of the story, which is then transformed into eighty pages and then into two hundred fifty. I do not do that. My books begin as books and grow from there. Right now I have one hundred thirty-two pages of a new novel, which I will not attempt to turn into one hundred eighty pages: they are what they are. There may be changes within these pages, but not the kind of changes that would be needed if I were working on a first draft of something that would eventually take on another form, either in length or in content. The alterations made are those needed for improvement, nothing more.

INTERVIEWER

So you begin writing with a concrete idea.

SARAMAGO

Yes, I have a clear idea about where I want to go and where I need to go to reach that point. But it is never a rigid plan. In the end, I want to say what I want to say, but there is flexibility within that objective. I often use this analogy to explain what I mean: I know I want to travel from Lisbon to Porto, but I don't know if the trip will be a straight line. I could even pass through Castelo Branco, which seems ridiculous because Castelo Branco is in the interior of the country—almost at the Spanish border—and Lisbon and Porto are both on the Atlantic coast.

What I mean is that the line by which I travel from one place to the next is always sinuous because it must accompany the development of the narrative, which might require something here or there that was not needed previously. The narrative must be attentive to the needs of a particular moment, which is to say that nothing is predetermined. If a story were predetermined—even if that were possible, down to the last detail that is to be written—then the work would be a total failure. The book would be obliged to exist before it existed. A book *comes into* existence. If I were to force a book to exist before it has come into being, then I would be doing something that is in opposition to the very nature of the development of the story that is being told.

INTERVIEWER

Have you always written in this way?

SARAMAGO

Always. I have never had another way of writing. I think this way of writing has permitted me—I am not sure what others would say—to create works that have solid structures. In my books each moment that passes takes into account what already has occurred. Just as someone who builds has to balance one element against another in order to prevent the whole from collapsing, so too a book will develop—seeking out its own logic, not the structure that was predetermined for it.

INTERVIEWER

What about your characters? Do your characters ever surprise you?

SARAMAGO

I don't believe in the notion that some characters have lives of their own and the author follows after them. The author has to be careful not to force the character to do something that would go against the logic of that character's personality, but the character does not have independence. The character is trapped in the author's hand, in my hand, but he is trapped in a way he does not know he is trapped. The characters are on strings, but the strings are loose; the characters enjoy the illusion of freedom, of independence, but they cannot go where I do not want them to go. When that happens, the author must pull on the string and say to them, "I am in charge here."

A story is inseparable from the characters who appear in it. The characters are there to serve the structure that the author wants to create. When I introduce a character, I know that I need that character and what I want from him; but the character is not yet developed—it is *being* developed. I am the one developing that character, but in a sense it is a kind of self-construction of that character, which I accompany. That is, I cannot develop the character against itself. I must respect the character or it will begin to do things of which it is not capable. For example, I cannot make a character commit a crime if it doesn't fall within the logic of that character—without that motivation, which is necessary to justify the act to the reader, it wouldn't make sense.

I will give you an example. *Baltasar and Blimunda* is a love story. In fact, if I may say so, it is a beautiful love story. But it was only at the end of the book that I realized I had written a love story without words of love. Neither Baltasar nor Blimunda speak any of those words to each other that we would consider words of love. The reader may think that this was planned, but it was not. I was the first to be surprised. I thought, How could this be? I have written a love story without a single amorous word of dialogue.

Now let us imagine that at some time in the future, in a reedition, I were to give into a whim to alter the dialogue between these two and insert a few words here and there: it would completely falsify those characters. I think the reader, even without knowing the book in its current form, would notice that something about this didn't work. How could these characters, who have been around each other since page one, suddenly say "I love you" on page two hundred and fifty?

That is what I mean by respecting the integrity of the character—not making him do things that would fall outside of his own personality, his internal psychology, that which the person *is*. Because a character in a novel is one more person—Natasha in *War and Peace* is one more person; Raskolnikov in *Crime and Punishment* is one more person; Julien in *The Red and the Black* is one more person—literature increases the world's population. We do not think of these three characters as beings who do not exist, as mere constructions of words on a series of sheets of paper that we call books. We think of them as real people. That is the dream, I suppose, of all novelists—that one of their characters will become "somebody."

INTERVIEWER

Which of your characters would you like to see as "somebody"?

SARAMAGO

Probably, I am committing the sin of presumption, but to tell the truth, I feel that all my characters—from the painter H. in *The Manual of Painting and Calligraphy*, to Senhor José in *All the Names (Todos os Nomes)*—are really somebody. I guess this is due to the fact that none of my characters is a mere copy—or imitation—of a real individual. Each one of them adds himself or herself to this world to "live" in it. They are fictional beings who lack only a physical body. This is how I see them, but we know that authors are suspect to being partial . . .

INTERVIEWER

For me, the doctor's wife in *Blindness* is a very specific person. I also have a specific visual image of her, as I do for all the characters in *Blindness*, despite the fact that there are no detailed descriptions of them.

SARAMAGO

It pleases me that you have a very exact visual image of her, which most certainly is not the result of physical descriptions of her, because there are none in the novel. I don't think it is worth explaining how a character's nose or chin looks. It is my feeling that readers will prefer to construct, little by little, their own character—the author will do well to entrust the reader with this part of the work.

INTERVIEWER

How did the idea for *Blindness* develop?

SARAMAGO

As has been the case with all of my novels, *Blindness* emerged from an idea that suddenly presented itself to my thoughts. (I am not sure this is the most precise formula, but I cannot find a better one.) I was in a restaurant, waiting to be served lunch, when suddenly, without any warning, I thought, What if we were all blind? As if answering my own question, I thought, But we really *are* blind. This was the embryo of the novel. Afterward, I only had to conceive the initial circumstances and allow the consequences to be born. They are horrific consequences, but they have a logic of steel. There is not much imagination in *Blindness*, just the systematic application of the relation of cause and effect.

INTERVIEWER

I liked *Blindness* very much, but it is not an easy read. It is a hard book. The translation is very good.

SARAMAGO

Did you know that Giovanni Portiero, my longtime English translator, died?

INTERVIEWER

When?

SARAMAGO

In February. He died of AIDS. He was translating *Blindness*, which he finished, when he died. Toward the end, he himself started to go blind as a result of the medication his doctors gave him. He had to choose between taking the medication, which would sustain him for a bit longer, and not taking it, which would create other risks. He chose, shall we say, to preserve his vision, and he was translating a novel about blindness. It was a devastating situation.

INTERVIEWER

How did the idea for *The History of the Siege of Lisbon* come about?

SARAMAGO

An idea had been with me since about 1972: the idea of a siege, as in a besieged city, but it was not clear who was besieging it. Then it evolved into a real siege, which I first thought of as the siege of Lisbon by the Castilians that occurred in 1384. I joined to this idea another siege, which occurred in the twelfth century. In the end, the siege was a combination of those two historical ones—I imagined a siege that lasted some time, with generations of besieged as well as generations of besiegers. A siege of the absurd. That is to say, the city was surrounded, there were people surrounding it, and none of this had a point.

In the end all of this came together to form a book that was, or that I wanted to be, a meditation on the notion of the truth of history. Is history truth? Does what we call history retell the whole story? History, really, is a fiction—not because it is made up of invented facts, for the facts are real, but because in the organization of those facts there is much fiction. History is pieced together with certain selected facts that give a coherence, a line, to the story. In order to create that line, many things must be left out. There are always those facts that did not enter history, which if they had might give a different sense to history. History must not be presented as a definitive lesson. No one can say, "This is so because I say it happened this way."

The History of the Siege of Lisbon is not a mere exercise in historical writing. It is a meditation on history as truth or history as a supposition, as one of the possibilities, but not as a lie even though it is often deceitful. It is necessary to confront official history with a *no*, which obliges us to look for another *yes*. This has to do with our own lives, with the life of fiction, with the life of ideologies. For example, a revolution is a *no*; that *no* is converted into a *yes*, either quickly or over time; so then it must be presented with another *no*. I sometimes think that *no* is the most necessary word of our times. Even if that *no* is a mistake, the good that could come from it outweighs the negative. *No* to this world as it is today, for example.

In the case of this book, it is far less ambitious—it is a small *no*, but it is still capable of changing one's life. By inserting a *not* in the sentence—the official history—that stated that the crusaders did assist the king of Portugal to reconquer Lisbon in 1147, Raimundo was not only led to write another history, but he also opened the way to changing his own life. His negation of that sentence is also a negation of his life as he was living it. That negation took him to another level of being; it removed him from his daily routine—from the grayness of his every day, his melancholy. He moves to another level and to the relationship with Maria Sara.

INTERVIEWER

Throughout *The History of the Siege of Lisbon*, both Raimundo and Maria Sara are presented as strangers—outsiders inside their own city. They even call each other Moors.

SARAMAGO

Yes, that's it. That is it. In the end, I believe that is how we all are.

INTERVIEWER

By *we* you mean the Portuguese?

SARAMAGO

Yes, but not only the Portuguese. All of us have to live in the city—I mean the city to be understood as a mode of living collectively—but at the same time, we should be outsiders, Moors, in that city—Moors in the sense that the Moor is simultaneously physically within the city and an alien to the city. It is because he is an outsider that he can effect change. The Moor, the other, the stranger, the strange one, shall we say, the one who despite being within the city walls is outside it, is the one who can transform that city—we hope in a positive sense.

INTERVIEWER

In the past you have been outspoken about your concerns about Portugal. What do you think about the present state of Portugal and its plan of integration into the European Union?

SARAMAGO

Let me give you an example. In an interview, João Deus de Pinheiro, who was our commissioner to the European Union, was asked by a Portuguese journalist, Don't you think that Portugal is in danger of losing much of its national sovereignty? His reply was, What do you mean *national sovereignty*? In the nineteenth century a Portuguese government did not take office because the admiral of the British fleet stationed in the Tagus River would not permit it. With that, he laughed. Should a country have a commissioner to the European Union who believes this historical episode to be amusing, and further that Portugal should not preoccupy itself with the loss of sovereignty because he believes we never actually had it?

If the European Union goes forward, then the responsibility of our politicians, as that of politicians of other countries, will diminish. From there they will become what fundamentally they already are: mere agents, because one of the great fallacies of our age is democratic discourse. Democracy is not working in this world. What is working is the power of international finance. The people involved in these activities in effect govern the world. The politicians are mere proxies—there is a kind of concubinage between so-called political power and financial power, which is the negation of true democracy.

People might ask me, "What do you propose instead?" I

propose nothing. I am a mere novelist, I just write about the world as I see it. It is not my job to transform it. I cannot transform it all by myself, and I wouldn't even know how to. I limit myself to saying what I believe the world to be.

Now, the question is, if I *had* to propose something, what would it be? I would propose what I have sometimes called *developing backwards*, which appears to be a contradiction, because one can only develop in a forward direction. *Developing backwards* means, very simply, this: the level we have reached—not the rich, but those in the upper middle class—allows us to live comfortably. *Developing backwards* would be to say, "Let us stop here and turn toward those billions of people who have been left behind." Of course, all this is utopian. I live in Lanzarote, an island with fifty-thousand inhabitants, and what happens in the rest of the world happens in the rest of the world. I do not aspire to be the savior of the world, but I live with the very simple belief that the world could be a better place, and it could very easily be made a better place.

This belief leads me to say that I do not like the world in which I live. The worldwide revolution I envision—please pardon my utopian vision—would be one of goodness. If two of us woke up and said, "Today, I will harm no one," and the next day said it again and actually lived by those words, the world would change in a short time. Of course, this is nonsense—this will never happen.

All this leads me to question the use of reason in this world. This is why I wrote *Blindness*. This is what has led me to a type of literary work that concerns itself with these issues.

INTERVIEWER

You have said that *Blindness* is the most difficult novel you've written. Is this because, despite the overt cruelty displayed by man toward his fellow man under the epidemic of white blindness, and the discomfort involved in writing about this behavior, you are ultimately an optimist?

SARAMAGO

I am a pessimist, but not so much so that I would shoot myself in the head. The cruelty to which you refer is the everyday cruelty that occurs in all parts of the world, not just in the novel. And we at this very moment are enveloped in an epidemic of white blindness. *Blindness* is a metaphor for the blindness of human reason. This is a blindness that permits us, without any conflict, to send a craft to Mars to examine rock formations on that planet while at the same time allowing millions of human beings to starve on this planet. Either we are blind, or we are mad.

INTERVIEWER

The Stone Raft also deals with social issues.

SARAMAGO

Well, it wasn't exactly the same, but people preferred to see it that way. People preferred to see it as the separation of the Iberian Peninsula from Europe. Of course, that is part of the story, and in fact that is what happens: the Iberian Peninsula separates itself from Europe and sails off down the Atlantic Ocean. But what I was getting at is not a separation from Europe, because that makes no sense. What I wanted to say and continue to say is what I believe to be the reality: Portugal and Spain have roots that are not exclusively European. I was saying to readers, "Listen, we have always been Europeans, we are Europeans and we will always be Europeans—there is no other way of being. But we have other obligations, obligations of an historical, cultural and linguistic nature. And so, let us not separate ourselves from the rest of the world, let us not separate from South America, let us not separate from Africa." This was not meant to reflect any neocolonial desires, but the Iberian Peninsula, as was the case in *The Stone Raft*, comes to rest between South America and Africa, and that happens for a reason. It is because we spend our lives speaking about the south, the south, the south, and the south has always been that place of exploitation, we could say, even when that south is located in the north.

INTERVIEWER

In your *Lanzarote Diaries* you write about your last trip to New York and say that in that city, the south is in northern Manhattan.

SARAMAGO

Yes, that south is located in the north.

INTERVIEWER

I have to tell you that I enjoyed your description of the Chelsea Hotel in the *Diaries*!

SARAMAGO

Oh, it was horrible. My publisher put me up there, but I still don't know exactly whose idea it was. They thought I had said that I wanted to stay there—but I never did say that. I knew the hotel from the outside, and I thought it was very attractive, but I never said, "Put me up at the Chelsea Hotel, please." I guess they put me there because it has a lot of history, but if I had to choose between an uncomfortable hotel with history and a comfortable one with no history . . . I kept saying to myself, "But what *is* this, I've never seen such a place."

INTERVIEWER

You have a wide readership in Europe and Latin America yet a small audience in the United States.

SARAMAGO

Things of too serious a nature don't really appeal to American readers. It is curious, however, that the reviews I receive in the United States are very good.

INTERVIEWER

Are the opinions of the critics important to you?

SARAMAGO

What is important to me is that I do my job well, according to my standards of what a good job is—that the book is written in the way I want it written. After it is out of my hands, it is just like everything else in life. A mother gives birth to a child and hopes the best for it, but that life belongs to the child, not the mother. The child will make of its life, or others will make of its life, something that most certainly will not be the life of which the mother dreamed. There is no use in my dreaming of magnificent receptions for my books by multitudes of readers because those readers will receive my books however they wish to.

I will not say that my books deserve to please readers because that would mean that the worthiness of a book depends on the number of readers. We know this to be untrue.

INTERVIEWER

During that trip to the United States, you also went to Fall River, an area of Massachusetts that has many Portuguese communities.

SARAMAGO

Yes, I had some contact with immigrants, those who for whatever reason were interested in my work. Surprisingly, I always had a good crowd, even though I am less and less interested in speaking about literature these days. I guess that would appear to be a contradiction because I write, and if I write books, what else should I speak about? Well I do write, but I was alive before becoming a writer and I had all the concerns of anyone else living in the world.

I was recently in Braga, Portugal, for a conference on my literary works, but we spoke about many other things—the situation in Portugal and what to do about it. I tell people that the history of the human race appears to be very complicated but actually it is extremely simple. We know that we live in a violent world. Violence is necessary to our species' survival: we have to kill animals, or someone has to kill them for us, in order for us to eat. We pick fruit; we even pick flowers to decorate our homes. These are all acts of violence carried out against other living beings. Animals behave in the same manner: the spider eats the fly, the fly eats whatever it is flies eat. However, there is one tremendous difference: animals are not cruel. When the spider wraps up the fly in its web, it is merely putting tomorrow's lunch in the refrigerator. Man invented cruelty. Animals do not torture each other, but we do. We are the only cruel beings on this planet.

These observations lead me to the following question, which I believe is perfectly legitimate: if we are cruel, how can we continue to say that we are rational beings? Because we speak? Because we think? Because we are capable of creating? Even though we are capable of all these things, it is not enough to stop us from doing all the negative and cruel things in which we engage. This is an ethical issue that I feel must be discussed, and it is for this reason that I am less and less interested in discussing literature.

Sometimes I think to myself, I hope we are never able to leave this planet because if we ever do spread out into the universe, it is not likely that we will behave differently there than we have here. If we could in fact inhabit the universe—and I do not believe we will be able to—we would infect it. We are probably a virus of some kind that fortunately is concentrated on this planet. I was recently reassured about all this, however, when I read about a supernova that had exploded. The light from the explosion reached the earth about three or four years ago—it had taken 166,000 years to arrive here. I thought, Well, there is no danger, we will never be able to go *that* far.

—Donzelina Barroso

Three Poems by David Wagoner

Thoreau Wading in a River

On summer days at the swampy edge of the river
He would bundle his shirt and shoes, his pantaloons
And drawers on the dry bank
And wearing only a wide-brimmed hat
Would begin his water walk, light-footed,
Feeling his way as deliberately
As a heron, at first upstream, even more slowly
Than the slow current against him, and with one hand
Would touch the lives of bedstraw and water starwort,
The open mouths of sundew, the radical leaves
Of floating heart, dull claret and green,
Pellucid in tufts and fringed
Like carrageen moss—all waders and waverers
That had learned to take the earth like him as it came
And went with the swells and fallings-away
Of wavelets and backwash. And at noon he would turn
And retrace his morning, sinking gradually
Deeper, seeing his feet like the undersides
Of flatfish taking their places calmly, surrounded
And then overcome by the dark debris and algae
Of the bottom, leaf mold, the empty houses
Of frog spawn, the casings of caddis larvae,
Among the castaway sheaths of ephemerella,
Of stoneflies, the husks of pondweeds melting
Under them, up through shallows a foot deep,
That would suddenly shelve and soften
Down into valleys till the surface rose
To circle his bare neck (the water as warm
As he was and as given to change), then to fall
To his breast, to his midriff, rippled

By all the piecemeal reflections
The sun could cast through branches, the fragments
Of its commentary on the passing order,
And through it, beyond it, midway
At his knees, the suspended blur of being
Held there, amiable as death, the wheeling
Cilia of rotifers in the living dust,
And see his body rise
As the bed rose to a surface thinning to nothing
And feel himself shedding the skin of the river,
Ready to wear again, as his own man,
The bundle of dry clothes there on the shore.

The Lessons of Water

The best way to conduct oneself may be observed in the behavior of water.

—Tao te ching

When given a place to wait, it fills that place
By taking the shape of what contains it,
Its upper surface poised and level,
Absorbing, accepting what it can as lightly
Or heavily as it does itself. If pressed
Down, it will offer back in all directions
Everything it was given. If chilled, it will shatter
Daylight and whiten to stars, will harden and sharpen
And turn unforeseeably dazzling. Neglected,
It will disappear, being transformed and lifted
Into thin air. Or thrown away, it will gather
With other water, which is all one water,
And rise and fall, regather and go on rising
And falling the more quickly its path descends
And the more slowly as it wears that path away,
To be left awhile, to stir for the moon, to wait
For the wind to begin again.

God and Man and Flower

Flower in the crannied wall,
I pluck thee out of thy crannies . . .
—Alfred, Lord Tennyson

But, my dear lord, now that it's in your hand,
What are you going to do with it? The roots
Of a windblown seed had groped sideways
Into flagstone crannies, grappling for root-holds
And root-room in a bent world. Its stem had come curving
Outward and upward from that bleak hardscrabble
Somehow poised, keeping its balance, to open
A small mouth to the light.

And now you've wrenched it loose, the sandgrains
And darker matter crumbling away from it,
And you hold it up to your nose, musing,
Then drop it into the gravel at your feet
Where it can wither and wilt at its leisure
While you continue your stroll, not understanding
What the flower knows: it is a terrible thing
To find yourself in the hands of the living god.

Sherod Santos

Elegy for My Sister

I

She was born *Sarah Gossett Ballenger*—
Sarah our mother's proper name, *Gossett* our mother's
family name, *Ballenger* the name of her father.
Following our mother's second marriage,
her name was changed to *Sarah Ballenger Santos*,
and when she herself got married, she became
Sarah Santos Knoeppel. After her divorce, she changed
her name to *Sarah Beth Ballenger*, though *Beth*
was selected simply because she "liked its sound,"
and because, for once, she'd felt entitled to name herself.

Following a stillbirth in the twelfth year
of her marriage, she instructed her daughters
to refer to her as *Mimi*—not *Mommy*, not *Mother*,
not *Mom*. At some point after she'd left home
(she was sixteen or seventeen at the time),
she changed the spelling of her familiar name
from *Sally* to *Salley*, and of her proper name
from *Sarah* to *Sara*, though here too the reasons
she gave were largely a matter of preference:
she just found those spellings more personal.

Thus all her life she felt her names referred to presences
outside of her, presences which sought to enclose
that self which separated *her* from who *they* were.
Thus all her life she was never quite sure who it was
people summoned whenever they called her by her name.
And, more specifically, she was never quite sure
they recognized *her* when, and if, she responded.

As she put it, at various periods in her life
she'd "lent" herself to particular names, only to reclaim
herself in time, only to suppose all over again.

II

. . . And so it is
I begin this now, a week after my sister's suicide,
because I can already feel her slipping beyond
the trace of words, and words, like bread crumbs
trailed behind her on the forest floor, are her way
back to us—or us to her—through the hemmed-in
reaches of the afterworld. But I begin this
for another reason as well. A more urgent
and perhaps more selfish reason, to answer
that question which day by day I fear
I'm growing less able to answer: *Who was she*
whose death now made her a stranger to me?
As though the problem were not that she had died,
and how was I to mourn her, but that some
stalled memory now kept her from existing.
And that she could only begin to exist,
to take her place in the future, when all of our
presuppositions about her, all of those things
that identified the woman we'd buried, were finally
swept aside. As if the time of her being
remained, as yet, a distant premonition within us.

III

Her hair was dark and irregularly parted,
and there was something undecided in the way
she chose to present herself to the world,
though her power over others (if not herself)
seemed to come from the confidence
of someone who felt she'd suffered more,
and so, perhaps rightly, assumed she possessed

the kind of spirit most favored by God.
But there was always something in the way
she dressed—an oversized brooch, a man's
sports watch, a garish hat or neckscarf—
which attempted to reverse that odd impression,
like those cowering dogs that so often appear
in seventeenth century religious paintings.
Those mongrel shapes that seem added to counter
some otherwise unabated spiritual yearning.

IV

As a rule, my sister didn't care for social gatherings,
though when she went she carried away
a palpable feeling of euphoria. This wasn't,
however, the euphoria of a "good time,"
but the accomplishment of someone who'd managed
to remain *incognito* under very exacting scrutiny.
When we were alone, this shyness proved self-
wounding, and I felt at times that many of the secrets
she confessed to me were things she actually
wished she regretted, more than things she suffered
for having done. In these and other respects,
she reminded me of those blue translucent birds
("so the hawks can't see them against the sky")
Marlon Brando describes in *The Fugitive Kind*.
Those legless birds that "don't belong no place
at all," and so stay on the wing until they die.

V

She was someone about whom people remarked:
She never seemed to find a life for herself. Or:
Her life was the story of a long collapse, its end
a dark, unlucky star she'd clung to hopefully,
for better or worse. Shortly after her death,
we discovered in her closet a large box containing

countless bottles of lotions, powders, lipsticks,
and oils. Many of them had never been opened,
still others had barely been used at all.
Sorting through the contents it occurred to me
the box contained some version of herself,
some representation of who she was—
a stronger? more serene? more independent self?—
that she'd never had the chance to become.
Sorting through the contents it occurred to me:
She once was becoming; she now ceased to become.

VI

Because of her "instability," doctors were reluctant
to write her prescriptions, though she was very adept
at describing those symptoms that called for the drugs
she wanted. She was also doggedly persistent.
One physician I telephoned defended his decision
by relating how, during one of her many unscheduled visits,
she'd remained in his office refusing to leave
until he'd written her a script for sleeping pills.
To be "cautious," he had written it out for only half
the normal number of pills. Which perhaps explains why,
on the floor beside her bed they found the empty vials
for four different drugs, each one ordered by
a different doctor—meprobamate, propoxyphene,
amitriptyline, and carisoprodol—a lethal combination
of anti-anxiety agents, painkillers, antidepressants,
and muscle relaxants. Clearly, killing herself
required the same cunning, and the same unspoken
complicity of others, that she'd needed to stay alive.

VII

Well, that what life's like. She'd say this
whenever she couldn't imagine what else
to say, or how her mind might disengage
that darkening shape-shift she could feel

was somehow, through her, handed down,
mother-to-daughter, daughter-to-child,
like the watercolors in her light-green eyes.
At the graveside, her two unkneeling daughters
closed in mute parenthesis around that space
(*Sarah Ballenger Santos Knoeppel*),
as if the soul encircled might recreate the ground
of being she'd unnamed; or lend new hope
to that vague impossibility: *Someone to love her*
for who she was. . . . A love I fear even she
finally felt incapable of when tears surprised
her stonewalled heart with what she'd done.

VIII

A dream I started having several weeks ago.
As in the newsreel of some dignitary-or-other
arriving in a foreign country, she's descending alone
the movable staircase from an airplane cabin,
and as she descends her face grows steadily younger
and more beautiful, like someone *coming into*
her own life. But instead of *the pathos of kindled hopes,*
I feel this moment as something that happens
to endanger her, something she is helpless to defend against,
as though the newsreel presaged an assassin's bomb.
This feeling brings with it a desperate urge
to "roll back the film," which succeeds only in slowing
it down to a pace that further accentuates the dread,
as though the newsreel'd slowed to capture the instant
the bomb goes off. Each step seems drawn out
endlessly, and falls so heavily on the heart
that I can feel—*in her*—the unearthly weight
a life takes on in the final moments it has to live.

IX

Is it inconceivable (I suspect this question haunts
us all) that all her life she was misunderstood?

That we'd shared a language which for whatever reasons
she herself had never learned? That all her attempts
to *draw us in* only further served to *hold us apart*?
That she'd had good reason to defend as *true*
what we'd perceived as *utterly false*? That what
she'd said in *love* or *affection* we'd heard as *confusion*,
anger, *fear*? Of course, these questions have no beginning
or end, and like posterity they fuel themselves
on a bottomless human vanity: the illusion that we can
know someone. Yet not to go on asking these questions
is to follow that line through time and space
that would lead us to experience her death (conclusively?
nostalgically? consolingly?) as "the final pages
of a novel." And how could she ever forgive us that?

X

My sister at thirty or thirty-one: stripping off table varnish
while her daughter naps on a folded towel beside her.

In the archangel section of the plaster cast gallery, she holds
her breath until the security guard stops looking her way.

On the table beside her bed: A bowl of dried wild roses
she would mist each morning with . . . was it rosewater?

Standing beside a photomat, staring at a strip of pictures, her look
of puzzlement slowly gives way to a look of recognition.

In the middle of the night—I was eight at the time—I wake
to find her patting my head, because *she* had just had a bad dream.

Her lifelong habit of momentarily closing her eyes, as if testing
the truthfulness of some emotion, then releasing a barely audible sigh.

Visiting hours over, her returning down the hall to her hospital room:
head down, shoulders stooped, her hands clasped behind her neck.

(That same morning, when she'd started to cry, she somehow managed
to distract herself by repeatedly crossing and uncrossing her legs.)

Overjoyed to be going home finally, then, mid-sentence, falling silent
at the thought of it, as though her mouth had been covered by a hand.

A warm spring night. A streetlamp beyond an open window.
Beneath the sill: a girl's hushed voice exhorting itself in whispers.

Honor Moore

A Window at Key West

Waking in silence and, through tilted blinds,
the mark of red bougainvillea—pink light tossed
at a white door. Out of sleep, I turn
in a narrow bed, and the sheet tugs after me.
Walls the color of milk, wind dragging leaves
across the courtyard, scraping whispers.
Life is incomprehensible, he'd said
when I asked if he had a theory. Late
dalliance of tropical green,
bromeliad, look of palm bark, and beyond

closed windows, a table set for supper.
In my dream I knock. A women offers spoiled food
then turns away. Now the sky goes dark
and the breeze stops. Why does she ask for narrative?
You make plans but sit instead on a porch
talking about Nietzsche whom you have
never read—never has sense seemed less
consequential. His skin is very black
against the white chair, his voice honest
and loose in the temperate air. The children

ask to walk, but we sink into a large car,
drive the quiet, small streets of an old town. This is
the shape my life takes around absence
any understanding would flatten. Light in the room,
but the sound is blocked—all that suggests it
is movement of light, shadow
rippling a surface of tawny wicker.
There are certain sentences I can't bear
to speak again: *I can love you less.*
Of course I understand. He brings plates of food—

green, then red, yellow. A red biplane, tall
glasses for beer, murmurs near a bar in shadow,
greeting without handshake or embrace;
then today in a room on the ocean, late silver
light, each chair a distinct bright color. He
asks only for the present: her face
behind a language I don't speak, something
pulling. Beyond a closed window the noise
of bodies in water, broken
by the talk of children. Her voice in this room

waylays almost any grief. Standing there
at an ironing board, the dress patterned and torn,
she burns her wrist: And so there will be
evidence. Later, wind and a raw Sunday heat: whites
go whiter, blacks blacken and glare until
eclipsed stripes of blind give actual
seconds of joy: red bougainvillea
the late light flushes almost blue, blossoms
folded to the shape of bells so
brilliant now, they seem to tremble and ring out.

Three Poems by V.S.M. Wang

The Gardener on Evisceration

What we have before us, obviously,
is the intestine. So why, you may wonder,
did I call you to the operating room
at this ungodly hour? Was it only to accustom you
to the sight of entrails piled on a groin
in limp wet folds? Was it rather
to demonstrate how to push the guts
back in gently so that they will simply
fall into place? Or was it, after all,
to let you who are ready see for yourselves
the wild flower bursting the seam?

Letter from a Homesick Traveler to a Fellow New Yorker

after Bishop

If you could only hear the chatter,
you would know how I was misled
earlier this morning when I woke
to the sound through open windows, ebbing
and flowing in the subtropical dampness,
of conversation in an unknown tongue.
It amazed me that my aunt's neighbors
had so much to say when the sun
had barely risen. But what language
were they speaking? I sat up
and listened, straining to recognize a word

or two. And then I knew—this
was the language of parrots. As I write,
they are still calling, one
to another, invisibly, from tree to tree.
Only slightly less foreign, the English words
fluttering with Australian accents
from a house below make me nostalgic
for the one language that held together
the bricks of the city—or at least
for the idea of one.
Across
the water, the houses, their roofs bright
with tiles of terra cotta, appear
to be rooted in the green hills as firmly
as native rocks. From the outside,
my aunt's house looks no different
from any other in Castlecrag,
a suburb of Sydney; but within,
it reverberates with the tones
of Chinese speech (I wanted to write
conversation, remembering just in time
that, according to the O.E.D.,
the word once conveyed the idea
of living in a particular place).
"Have you heard that the dim sum
here and in New York is better,
in fact, than what you find in Hong Kong
nowadays?" My mother and her sister
are in the kitchen wrapping wontons
for lunch, sealing the edges with water,
then folding the ends together
behind. They sprinkle their talk
with grated English—both the Australian
and the American varieties. Ignored,
the pet cockatoo is greeting herself
with a "Hello, Cookie!" or unfolding the fan
of her yellow crest while demanding,

in Chinese, to know what all
the fuss is about.
I, too,
would like to know where all these words
are taking us. How can I capture
for you, in a single language, the flavor
of the talk around the kitchen table
or make myself at home in one
particular tongue? Perhaps it is futile
to try. Perhaps I will never be able,
anyway, to describe the fragrance
of the local mangoes. Yet, viewed
from this terrace, the Tor Walk
becomes, for a moment, a nameless street
anywhere. There are even a few stalks
of bamboo behind the house. Fluently,
the wild cockatoos continue their wordless
conversation. And I envy them.

Your Offering

The whole hollow globe of orange, balanced
where ashes usually fall, in the crystal
curve of the ashtray, brightened the table.

You called it a poetic metaphor; and what you saw,
no doubt, was a metaphor for poetry—a spiral
of orange peel arranged to look like fruit.

Indeed, the rind you had posed in the ashtray was
empty, but only because you had swallowed
its juice, pulp, and even the seeds.

Kim Mattson

May Day 1986

Everything on the outside is the same this morning. On the
  outskirts of Kiev,
our farmland overturned, the cows' mouths grinding in
  silent motion.

Across the table, he stares: *You must promise me.* Lids
  burdened
with a scientist's insight. Around his mouth tight lines draw
  willful fingers, instruct,
forget what you know, forbid
                                        everything he has told me.

Atomic lesion. For days, a white-hot graphite fire
  unquenchable, swelling: black clouds
churning epidemic. When will they tell the people? Words
  are husks, vomit.

Even here, hours from the explosion, nausea. My thoughts
  turning
to visions of babies with limbs knotted, eyes sealed shut.
  Could I somehow betray him?
Nothing remains now, is mine. What I say folds over itself
  like water in a cistern.

Curtains drawn. A clear film scrubbed from our lashes,
  our fingernails.
Eyes hollow, he turns from the television
                                                    while behind
  him in Red Square
crowds cheer as Gorbachev steps to the platform: celebration
  of spring

and the worker—the scientist: locked in obligation. I turn
  down the lamp.
Wrapped in our quilt, layers and folds of warmth . . .
  the windows haze
as chalky voices grow nearer. Soon uniforms and fists raised
  to the door will take him
from sleep, in the way of Sakharov and Gertsen, and I will
  go with him.

Morning rises purple, in secret. Everywhere it leaks
into day and I have forgotten everything. The air is blue:
  stalks of poison.

Beth Gylys

Marriage Song

They have affairs. They rarely stop to think
until they're begging for a second chance.
We love and learn we sometimes need a drink.

Impatient with his life, he quipped, "We blink
we're forty: with wives, kids, retirement plans."
They have affairs. It isn't what we think.

He saw this woman at the skating rink,
watching their sons play hockey from the stands.
He fought the urge to ask her for a drink.

She wore those stretchy pants, a long faux mink,
slid next to him and said, "Hi, my name's Nance."
He wanted her right there. He couldn't think.

They fucked in hotel rooms, designer pink,
drank cheap champagne. He signed her underpants.
They fucked and ordered something else to drink.

His wife broke all the dishes in the sink,
took both the kids and flew first-class to France.
They have affairs—it's never what they think.
We sigh and shake our heads. We have a drink.

Indians

Jon Billman

Like all prolonged natural disasters, the Dakota dust bowl bred superstition. Real estate changed hands by the bushel. The government and railroad boosters had told dirt-poor eastern farmers that if they moved into the Great American Desert and plowed, the rains would come. But unlike the chinch bugs, rain had not followed the plow here. After the buffalo were gone, the cattle ate the buffalo grass down to nothing. Then came the barbed-wire fences that only wind and soil and grasshoppers could pass through. After a few good wet years the droughts came. Then more mice and rabbits and winds. Without asking, folks in the Dakotas got parts of Texas and Oklahoma, and Canada landed good Dakota bottomland for a whistle. Townships, counties, entire states began to hold collective days of prayer to try to coax God into ending the suffering. It was a form of spiritual cloud-seeding as well as a one-ring circus. Preachers wrung their hands, looked at their shoes, then at the sky. People's new hope was that beating the socks off an Indian ball team might change the medicine.

We spent most of the Depression as barnstormers, living like the hoboes who packed the boxcars thick as blackbirds, and playing other Indian League reservation teams, civic all-stars, semipro teams, barnstorming colored squads, CCC teams, Rotarians and prison teams for whatever beans, chickens, Grain Belt beer and gasoline we could get.

We drove around the Dakotas with the windows open, our mouths shut against the dirt that would settle on our molars. Sometimes the dust would be so bad we had to keep wet handkerchiefs over our faces to breathe. When we were playing well and did have the money, we weren't allowed in most hotels or motor lodges. We stayed in the colored motels, but those were rare in the plains. Usually we stopped the car and slept with fleas and chiggers on wool blankets under the stars. Never rained anyway.

Our pitcher Job Looks Twice could tell the weather in his sleeve. "Hot today," he'd say when we set out in the old Model T for another town. Waves of heat rose from the hood of the car. Dust rolled in the open windows and stuck to our faces. "Very hot." It was in the last of the wet years that Job, drunk as nine Indians, had fallen asleep on the tracks in downtown Sioux City, giving his right arm to a loaded east-bound grain train.

Not only could they not reattach his arm, but they never found it. For a time, just after the accident, Job cursed God and prayed that he might die. But the stump healed without infection and unlike the rest of the country, Job's personal depression was short-lived. He cropped his hair, bought a new black traveling suit and straw fedora, and—good thing he pitched from the port side—went on to keep us well above .500. This in 1931 when it wouldn't rain any real amount on the plains for another ten years. Dust was a part of our lives.

Job was a second-generation product of the missionaries and, after the accident, became obsessed with repentance. The loss of the limb had thrown the big lefty off balance just enough to make his curveball dance and his slider tail slick and hard. With the stump that began just above where his elbow had been before Sioux City, he cradled his left-handed, three-fingered glove against his chest. He released the ball, followed through with his good arm and capped the glove onto his good hand before the pitch reached the strike zone.

Job could field bunts as well as shots rifled at the mound, though he didn't need to have much range as a fielder: the other Indians—Asa Red Owl, Carp Whitehorse, Baptist Thundergrass, Walter and Jacob Elk, Jeremiah "Big Chief" Montgomery, Otis Downwind and I—covered the field like a trade blanket. At the plate Job learned to bunt one-handed and usually beat the throw to first.

In those days farmers and bankers would search the dawn sky for signs of rain, but the only clouds were clouds of dust, the only storms the soil-and-wind rollers that blew out of the south and west. "We cannot expect to understand the mysteries of God's weather," Job would say. He believed everything happened for a reason, God's reason, and unlike the rest of the team, Job never tried to question the logic behind the reason.

Besides his beloved spitball, Job was partial to another illegal gem he called his "needleball." At any general store you could buy 78 rpm phonograph needles fifty for a dime. Job kept a few of the needles stuck at arm length in the seams of his trousers and a dozen or so more behind the mound under his rosin bag. With a motion that looked like he was simply wiping his only hand, he would unquiver a needle and finger it into the threads of the ball. The weight of the needle put rising zip onto his fastball and a ten-inch break in his nickel curve. Umpires would examine the ball but never find anything because the impact with the mitt or bat knocked the needle from the seams and into the dirt.

Before his accident Job's needleball had nearly killed a white man over in Woonsocket. The guy had used his spikes on Baptist Thundergrass at second base in the first inning and Job had been brushing him back all afternoon with a salvo of knockdowns at the chest. Job would get the batter nervous and deep in the box, then paint the outside corner for strikes. A fastball in the eighth got away and he caught the batter in the temple. The man appeared dead, but as it turned out, Job only blinded him.

The Woonsocket players, too stunned to charge the mound, hovered around their downed comrade, fanning dust away from his nostrils. A minister climbed out of the stands and stood over the body, saying a prayer for his soul. Big Chief Montgomery walked out of a dirt devil in right field and started the car while the newly blind man held everyone's attention. The Indians lit out of town under cover of a dust storm. Blind man couldn't do more than snap beans for a living after that. Ever after the Indians steered clear of Woonsocket.

When Job lost his arm to the grain train, he thought it was retribution for the blinding. Arm for an eye. Job believed that if he lived a good life his derailed arm would be waiting for him when he died.

"Sometimes," he said, "I'll reach for something with the arm that's not there. A tin cup. A baseball. I can feel the thing but can't pick it up. Then I'm aware that it will not be raining anytime soon." Job was sure weather came from heaven. "If my good outweighs the not-good and I make it there, I'll get my arm back. And the blind man from Woonsocket will get his eyes."

As boys, we had an old horsehide ball my father, a missionary from Sioux Falls, had given us. Though I was white and Presbyterian as hell, I had hair black as a crow. I wore it long and braided. I tanned like a buffalo hide under the sun. My father's lifework was to save the heathen from the fires of damnation. When the Indians took to barnstorming, I chose baseball over Jesus, packed my Sunday suit in a canvas satchel, and set out for the open prairie with the Everywhere Spirit.

We had grown up together in Porcupine, playing prairie ball on a sand and rock field in the cool of early evening. When the Cubs and White Sox games were on and the weather allowed for good reception, we would sit cross-legged in the mercantile owned by Asa's mother and listen through the static on a storage-battery neutrodyne set to the Chicago teams on WLS. The nine of us, shiny black hair, no shirts, dirty bare feet, sat on the oiled pine floor and stared at the radio among the canned goods. The radio put the idea of professional baseball into our heads. We would play ball, passing around our one and only glove, taking turns spitting Red Man chaw into the sweet spot and working it in with our fists. We learned to field bad hops bare-handed, bad hops being the rule.

Job stayed out past dark every night, throwing at a red strike zone painted on an outhouse behind the store. Throw, walk, pick up the ball, back to the makeshift mound, throw again at the target he could no longer see. Job's pitching made a slow, metered thump against the weathered wood like the beating of a drum at sunset.

I began to stay behind with him to catch, where the whistling sound of his pitches became so familiar that soon I could catch Job in the dark. Though I was small and skinny, I grew to realize that my place in life was to wear the secondhand tools of ignorance in the dirt behind home plate. "How's the arm tonight?" I'd yell to Job, knowing he wouldn't answer. His mind was too busy listening to the electric hum of his pitches.

We got the red and gray wool flannel uniforms, patched and stained, but free, from a women's relief circle over in Mud Butte. The uniforms were at least ten years old, having belonged to a team of white ranch hands. The team name came easy—the felt letters across the chest already scripted: MUD BUTTE INDIANS.

The Indians' play had much in common with the colored teams of the time. We were hustlers. We liked to bunt. We loved to steal third and home. We utilized the squeeze play, and the hit-and-run. We knew about sacrificing.

Sometimes our aggressiveness cost us runs. But often, against the better teams—colored teams and semipro squads out of Aberdeen or Jamestown or Dickinson or Mobridge or Chadron or Stillwater—we often made up the difference between losing and winning through hustle alone. This with only an hour or two of bad sleep in the car and just nine players—no one on the pine. Job Looks Twice had to pitch the entire game and even double headers some Sundays. Sometimes the winning was so easy we put one of the Elk brothers on the mound to rest Job's arm. Some days we played our hearts out and won. Other days a different luck would pick up a bat and knock us into the next county.

Close calls always went to the other team. Called strikes were unheard of. Job never argued with umpires because he knew it was fruitless. The umps had the support of the fans, who sometimes resembled angry mobs. The other teams either had to go down swinging or hit the ball into play so we could glove it.

Our vested interest in winning games went well beyond pride. When we didn't win we didn't get paid. We were in high demand. Our name was hoodoo. Many people believed that beating the Indians would bring a break from the dust. As well as being the catcher, I also arranged the Indians' schedule, which usually meant wiping the layers of dust from my face, tucking my braid down the back of my collar and hustling into town while the rest of the Indians scrounged up supper by the river. Except for Job. We'd find the local watering hole and speak with the mayor, the sheriff, barkeeps, the undertaker, the men who planned the games. They ran ads in the local newspapers, cartoons of feathered savages with big teeth and tomahawks running bases. Word of our winning preceded us and opposing teams shot beanballs at our heads in the early innings. Sometimes it was a hard sell to get the men interested in playing us at all. "Beat us and maybe it will rain," I told them, their eyes on Job and the arm that wasn't there. *Hell*, their faces would say, *if we can't beat a one-armed Indian baseball team, we don't deserve rain*.

"You shouldn't sell us on rain," Job said to me once on the way back to the river camp. "It will come back to hurt us."

"Sometimes it's the only way I can sell us," I said. The more I sold the Indians as Rainmakers, the less Job accompanied me to town, until finally he stopped altogether.

Just before the Indians lost Job to the weather for good, we played an honest-to-God rainmaking in Custer and won under a hot, cloudless sky. The pine woods around Custer were terribly dry and infected with beetles, and fire threatened to flatten the entire town. Heavy woodsmoke from the lumber kilns hung in the brown trees like a premonition. The mill boss let his employees off on a Wednesday afternoon for the game and townsfolk took a desperation holiday. Custer also had gotten word that beating the Indians would bring rain. The Indians beat the Colonels 7 to 0. We were glad for the victory and downright thankful to make it out of town with our hides. They were too mad that we took away their rain to bother paying us. These white towns took their water rights seriously. It was a long time thereafter before Custer got rain.

We kept winning games and it kept not raining. Sometimes we got paid, but most often not. Job began believing in the pattern of winning and no rain, no matter how hard we tried to talk him out of it. "I know the weather," he said, gripping his empty sleeve.

"Maybe it is true," Job said to me after the Custer win. "You say it when you go to town."

"I only say it so they'll want to play us. It's business," I tried to reason.

"We won the game, and I know the weather," he said, gripping his empty sleeve. "There is no rain."

"Times are hard," Otis Downwind said. "Back in Winner I saw a porcupine behind the roadhouse eating on a onion."

"So what?"

Otis looked at Job and paused. "Times are hard when a porcupine's gotta eat a onion."

After a few more non-paying, no-rain wins, when things were looking especially hungry for the Indians, I managed to set up a rainmaking game in Faith, with a couple of other games along the way. We spent the next few days in the car, heading into the setting sun, to Faith, at a bone-jarring thirty miles per hour.

The car wasn't a thing to rely on. The best Model Ts lasted about thirty-five thousand miles. Ours had over fifty thousand miles when Asa bought it from an old man in Mitchell. The car handled the rutted dirt roads like a cattle car. The wind and dirt had sandblasted the paint off and the body was rusted nearly through. Now and then it would backfire—kaboom!—loud as a field gun. For relief from the heat we hung canvas water bags from the door hinges. Condensation formed and made the air blowing over the bags less hot. When the radiator boiled over—which happened every fifty or so miles with the load of us—the bags came in handy. Some days it started. Other days it didn't.

Tumbleweeds collected along the fencerows and dirt drifted against the tumbleweeds until it almost covered the fences. What grass was left burned. Smoke filled the sky and we never truly did see it blue. Some days, through the haze, a dirt roller would birth out of the horizon. It looked like a thunderstorm, but blacker, angrier. Sometimes the Indians would be on a ball field, sometimes we'd be in the middle of nowhere in the Ford. The sun would disappear altogether and there'd be midnight at noon.

On the way to the rainmaking we stopped to wash our uniforms and feet with rocks and powdered soap in a shallow, muddy slew of the Bad River. Job loved to fish for catfish. He would bait his hook with a grasshopper at the end of a braided line on an old cane pole he carried strapped to the car like an antenna. Some folks who had already lost everything lived along the rivers in Hoover camps. They fished for food and when the carp and catfish weren't biting there was no dinner. Out of canned hams and beets, our guys hadn't eaten since early the day before when we'd caught a few bluegills and Job beaned a rain crow with a fastball. We roasted the pigeon-tasting bird over the campfire and ate it with coffee.

The next day Job landed a channel cat that must have gone fifteen pounds. He picked up the fish by the lip and walked to a little camp of tents that met with the river and the highway. He gave the cat to a family of sharecroppers with eight or ten young kids.

"What in hell," said Carp Whitehorse. "You gave them our dinner for nothing?"

"Not for nothing," Job said, shaking his stump at the third baseman. "Nothing is for nothing."

Our uniforms dried flapping in the wind on the long drive to Faith.

The Indians blew into Faith from the east. I slowed the car and idled down Main Street to the ball field at the west end of town, near the sun-bleached Lutheran church. Folks on the square pointed and stared. A brass band warmed up with scales in a weathered gazebo.

The outfield in Faith was dirt, cracked and hard, just like the infield. Barbed wire separated center from the scrabbled wheat field where brown and yellow shoots of Russian wheat gasped for water and fought to stay upright. This wheat held hope. As Job threw me some lifeless pitches and the rest of the Indians played pepper and stretched, the bleachers slowly filled with baseball fans, the convicted and the simply curious.

"How's the arm tonight?" I yelled to Job.

"Which one?" Job said.

There was at the time a white barnstorming team from a religious settlement up in Michigan called the House of David. They let their hair and beards grow long and godlike and kept Bibles with them in the dugout. We had met them on the road before, at chautauquas and county fairs, and respected them because, yes, they preached humbly to the fans before the games, but after the first pitch their spirits were real. Their fervor for God turned into a fervor for baseball and winning. They cursed like Philistines in their blue and gray uniforms and threw at batters' heads. A Whisker—pitcher named Benson—eventually made it to the Bigs. The games were as intense as firefights. It was like facing Jesus at every position.

This game would be our first-ever night game. Crude portable lights were trucked in along with generators. The steel stanchions were short and the lights yellow and not very bright, creating shadows behind everything. It made possible an incandescent noon at midnight. To folks in those parts, and even to us, a night baseball game was a miracle.

Farmers and the CCC crews were all off from work and gathered in town at dinnertime to eat and talk about baseball and the changeless weather. Horses and mules pulled wagon loads of children. A Methodist church had set up an old army tent and a choir practiced and sipped iced tea. Faith had the feel of the chautauqua.

The crowd watched us take infield practice. Hope and desperation played on their faces—babies crying, mothers crying, fathers cursing and praying in the same breaths. They cheered our mistakes while grasshoppers danced in the dusky light that filtered through the dust. Ministers and deacons in dark suits and straw hats passed walnut collection plates.

From the tin lean-to visitors' dugout, we watched the Whiskers take infield. "I have felt weather in my arm all day," Job said while fishing the June bugs from the water bucket with the drinking gourd. "Tonight there will be weather." The air was heavy with humidity. Heat lightning flashed to the west. "We will be rewarded with God's prosperity."

In the hazy twilight, both teams racked up errors involving lack of sight. As it got darker we played blind to the balls that were hit over the lights, which were many. Line drives hid in the lights and the outfielders had to react to directions from their infielders. We communicated with whistles, growls and shrieks only the Indians understood. Even Job's breaking balls were hard to pick up in the shadows, and I had to track them through the sound of the batter's breathing.

The Indians hit the ball hard and put runners on base all evening. Except for Job, who seemed to have lost a step in beating the throw to first. But we did score runs, even driving two long balls in the wheat, one with two aboard.

The umpiring had been stacked against the Indians from the very beginning. The umps were Faith Rotarians who didn't see any benefit in another Indian coup. Job couldn't get a called strike, and most of his pitches lacked snap and heat, and the Whiskers spent the evening whacking breadbasket strikes into the outfield and sometimes beyond. I knew Job was convinced that throwing the game would be an offering of something more important than the purse money we would never see, a tithe of weather that would bring the Indians something more. Losing would mean rain, a final truce. Job believed he could control the hellish dry spell and its curse on all the land. He was now willing to lose on purpose—a personal sacrifice that he believed with all his soul would bring a saving rain. The other eight of us weren't convinced and wanted to beat the Whiskers like a drum.

Job kept shaking off the pitches I called, hurling instead easy fastballs, sliders that didn't slide and change-ups that weren't much of a change. In the fourth I started to the mound to talk some sense into him, but how do you avoid a sermon at a time like that? Our eyes met. He pointed at the storm cell that was building over the Black Hills to the west. I realized I had nothing to say to him that would matter and walked back to my crouch behind the plate. More slow fastballs.

But the Indians battled hard at the plate as well. A pitching duel this wasn't. Both teams batted around two innings in a row.

Indians were up one at the bottom of the ninth, thirteen to twelve, Whiskers on first and second, two out. From his one-armed stretch Job checked the runners. Then again. He shook off my signs until we agreed on a fastball. His eyes were yellow and sorry, like the chiefs on old tobacco cans.

He hadn't licked his fingers or gone to the rosin bag or the seam of his pants for a phonograph needle all game.

Then Job put a dull fastball into the wheelhouse of Joe Garner, the Whiskers' cleanup man. Garner stepped into the bucket, swung through and massacred the easy mushball. A rainmaker. Otis Downwind in left ran underneath it just to say good-bye. The stitched horsehide that Job had always said possessed the spirit of the horse was still traveling skyward into the humidity when the wind came fast and quiet, ambushing the ball, pulling it down into the surprised glove of Otis Downwind, and ending the game.

From my knees in the dirt—the knees I can feel the big storms with now—I could hear the wall of wind coming toward the diamond like a night train. Loud claps of thunder boomed just west of center field. Lightning struck the prairie with a dozen electric arrows. "Smell the rain!" the crowd yelled. "The miracle! Do you smell the rain! At last, thank God, the rain!"

The crowd stood, frozen. For a moment, the Indians too were transfixed by the rush of wheat under the black umbrella of clouds. Then, silently, eight of us ran off the field to the car, Otis desperately throwing himself into the crank, trying to turn the engine over.

"Job, come on!" I yelled over the wind, but he didn't move, didn't even turn to look at us. By now, everyone but Otis and me were piled in the car.

The crowd reached to touch the weather, and Job, still on the mound, face to the sky, waved his gloved hand and stump in the air in exaltation. Thunder cracked as the engine fired up and the crowd yelled louder. The car sputtered slowly away from the field, picking up speed toward the dirt highway, as Otis and I ran beside it, still calling for Job.

The storm rolled eastward across the prairie, towards Faith, with the sound of a thousand horses racing to the river as the wheat was beaten with hailstones the size of baseballs.

Ilya Kabakov

Anthony Haden-Guest

Ilya Kabakov was a central figure in the tiny world of Moscow's unofficial artists, meaning artists who did not hew to the party line and who were constantly harassed by the authorities, the most malign, of course, being the KGB. By the time he came to live in America in 1988, Kabakov was well-known in the art world of the West for his installations—works that exist in three dimensions, but are environments (often ephemeral) rather than sculptures, and can include sound, and God knows what. The mode has a sketchy history—it includes such work as the garbage assembled by the Dada artist Kurt Schwitters—but it wasn't until the seventies that installation became part of the art-world repertoire big-time. Ilya Kabakov is one of the rare figures to have taken this mode and used it to make great art.

Typical of Kabakov's brooding "total installations" was The Toilet, *a lavatory stall occupied by a make-believe family of street people, which he built for the documenta exhibition, Kassel, Germany, in 1992. The following year, he took the old Soviet pavilion in the Giardini and wrecked it, turning it into a shell haunted by its imperial socialist past. At the 1997 Whitney Biennial, he turned a segment of the top floor into* Treatment with Memories, *a somber hospital wing. To walk through a Kabakov installation, preferably when it is fairly unpeopled—no easy thing on the museum-gallery circuit, of course—is somewhat like immersing yourself in a play or a novel. Swept in, you are aware of the strangeness of your surroundings, but the rushes of emotion that are triggered are private, and familiar.*

There is more to the artist's oeuvre than installations. Kabakov, who went through the rigorous beaux arts training of the Soviet era, and who has supported himself by illustrating childrens' books, is also a master of the lost art: drawing. Indeed, Kabakov was working with drawings when I went to his Manhattan studio this fall. He has a broad face, which crinkles when he smiles, and seems both sagacious and kindly. Emilia Kabakov, the artist's wife, a woman with a fine face and hair cropped fashionably short, was on the telephone. The studio is a trim, austere space, all pale and gleaming wood, with neatly piled cardboard boxes and archival materials. It seems a world away from the Kabakovs' former Moscow studio, which is being devoutly maintained by a small arts group as if it were a monument to the undercover world of the avant-garde in the old Soviet Union. Which, of course, is just what it is.

INTERVIEWER

I recently went to your old studio in Moscow. I asked them if Mr. Kabakov ever comes back? They said no.

ILYA KABAKOV

When did you go?

INTERVIEWER

About ten months ago. Can you imagine going back there?

KABAKOV

I have no reason.

INTERVIEWER

No reason? But your work deals so much with time, with memory, that it might be almost like Proust eating the madeleine for you to go back.

KABAKOV

That's the reason I can't go back. Because the memory is now imagination, and the reality is going to be very different.

INTERVIEWER

When did you start making drawings for the children's books?

KABAKOV

I started doing it when I was in the Art Institute in 1955. But it doesn't mean that I love children's books or that I love children. I wanted to do my paintings. But I really knew that my paintings would be different and nobody would want them. So in order to make money I had to make books. Artists had to live a double life. One main part of our life was for ourselves and our friends and the other was to make a living. I spent some time making money and some time making what I wanted. For my friends, it was necessary to work six months making money and for six months making art for themselves. For me, I was lucky. I managed to do it in a shorter time. Three months money-making.

INTERVIEWER

I love nineteenth-century children's book illustrations. Tenniel's illustrations for the Alice books, for instance. It's not to do with children. It's to do with imagination. I think I see some of that in your work.

KABAKOV

The problem was that in Russia, the Soviet Union, it was a different situation with children's books. There was very strong censorship and many demands on how to do the stories in children's publishing. The censorship was not only on the text but also on the images. You had to work according to standards. Have you seen a rabbit perform in the circus? It doesn't mean the rabbit loves to perform in the circus.

INTERVIEWER

I remember visiting the Tretiakov Museum during the eighties and being surprised to see a few pieces, mostly plates and theater designs by the Suprematists.

The Tretiakov is Moscow's modern museum, but during the Communist period would show only official—meaning state-approved—artists. The Suprematists, a group inspired by Kazimir Malevich, were an avant-garde group of the early revolutionary period, and Malevich painted arguably the first truly abstract paintings. Like Russia's other avant-gardes, they were extirpated under Stalin. Malevich ended up doing folksy images.

KABAKOV

At the time when I was studying, it was absolutely impossible to see the Suprematists. Our artistic education ended with the Barbizon School.

INTERVIEWER

When did you first see the work of Malevich?

KABAKOV

Malevich was never exhibited when I was in Russia. In the unofficial world we tried to get books and productions, but it was very difficult. Sometimes possible. So I think I was seeing it in the seventies.

INTERVIEWER

I visited the Hermitage in St. Petersburg. What they have done is interesting. One modern corridor is hung with the great moderns. The other is hung with what you would have seen in Communist times. They didn't act like Stalinists and pack the unfashionable stuff in the basement.

KABAKOV

What was before the bottom is now the top. And what was the top is now the bottom.

INTERVIEWER

When did you make your first installation?

KABAKOV

1984.

INTERVIEWER

You were already here?

KABAKOV

No, no, no. Moscow. In general, I was doing projects that were realized in the West. Some of the installations were realized for the first time in Switzerland. But without my presence, because I couldn't at the time leave Russia. Some installations I was making at my studio in Moscow, and would invite my friends to look at them.

INTERVIEWER

What attracted you to the form?

KABAKOV

Before installations I was making drawings, paintings. Because we didn't have any contact with the West or any knowledge of Western art, making installations was part of my inner evolution. Maybe because of my personal circumstances I lost interest in painting. And I was interested in doing something in three-dimensional space—something that would surround the viewer. Later, when I came to the West, I found out that the installation form already existed. So I had no difficulty in making them.

INTERVIEWER

Many artists prefer materials that defy time, like bronze and marble. Your work is full of time and memory. Yet because of the form you have chosen, much of it will only exist in memory.

KABAKOV

It is not only my problem. It is the problem of anybody who works in installations. There are great problems with making installations. Museums don't want to buy them because they take up too much space. And collectors! One collector told me, "It's beautiful and I really want it, but it's only going to survive until my next wife." It's a paradox. The work will continue, and will live, in spite of all the problems. In spite of all the difficulties. I am a fanatic.

INTERVIEWER

How did you come up with your very first installation before you knew artists in the West were exploring the form?

KABAKOV

In my fantasies, inside of myself, I saw a work that the viewer somehow could enter. I wanted the viewer to become completely involved with the work, to experience the work. Art, as I understand it, is a different world. The viewer must be able to participate. This used to be the role of painting. The viewer would enter the frame of the painting and enter this other world—angels, paradise. He will lose himself in this world. But five hundred years have passed and painting has simply lost these abilities. I think that installation right now has the same project.

INTERVIEWER

So walking into one of your pieces is like walking into an old church. You borrow from theater, you borrow from literature.

KABAKOV

The viewer has to encounter not only the world of art but the world that he already knows very well. The world of his childhood, his teachers, his bed when he was sick. There are elements that will be recognizable by any citizen of any country. They are universal. Fear, helplessness, hope.

INTERVIEWER

Your faith in the imagination does seem Russian, though. I am reminded a bit of Andrei Tarkovsky's film *Stalker*. And of Ciolkowsky, revered as the father of Soviet rocketry, who also believed that we would ultimately evolve into radiant beings, traveling through space in our own bodies.

KABAKOV

Yes. It's very Russian. We could say that the whole right wing in Russia is provoking a movement of dreams and fantasies. But they want to get as far from reality as possible. The West does not understand. There are two different types of existence. In the West, people are living. In Russia, they are surviving. And in a situation of survival dreams are enormously important.

INTERVIEWER

You are off to Germany now to work on a monument?

KABAKOV

Bremerhaven. There was a competition. Bremerhaven was a port from which emigrants left for America. There is an old building where they stayed.

This commission, which is to commemorate a prior wave of emigration, clearly excited Kabakov. He opened a drawer, produced a sheaf of color-Xeroxed drawings. They show the building, which is of oxblood-colored brick, and the internal murals he will be, yes, painting. They turn the room into a ship with a tilting deck.

KABAKOV

It will be graffiti, in fresco. Like a ghost! Like an old painting. In the front of the ship it is possible to see New York. That will be the future.

INTERVIEWER

After George Grosz (the German artist who became a US citizen in 1938) had been in this country a while, he began producing very America-inflected art. Will you be using American material in your work?

KABAKOV

For the last three years, I have been doing very different work. And there is an enormous amount of work that is already not connected with Russia. It's the work that is strongly connected with the soul and the contents of the space.

INTERVIEWER

Of course, a huge number of people in New York, myself included, originally come from somewhere else.

KABAKOV

For instance, the *Monument to the Lost Glove*. It was standing for a year on Twenty-fourth Street. That has nothing to do with Russia. The reaction of New York people was incredible. Every time I would go to check it, I would see concerts . . . young students would be making music.

I am not authoritarian. I am not interested to show in every place pieces specifically done by me. My voice is a minor part of the work. I am much more interested in communicating with the viewer and the reactions of the viewer. The others are more interesting. You construct information in such a way that you will touch the viewer—touch his spirit like music does. They are your own things, but the viewer has to be able to think that it is about him as well.

The Monument to the Lost Glove, *which was erected by New York's Public Art Fund, stood on the traffic triangle just opposite the Flatiron Building. Kabakov writes texts to accompany his installations. The text he wrote for the* Glove *lets you know that the piece was inspired by a red plastic glove lost beside a jogging track. It is in nine voices. One begins lyrically:*

> A red spot on green—a strong, bright hit, what freshness.
> Oh, how the entire landscape resounds from this spot on the grass!

This voice ends with a longing backwards look to Monet, Pissarro, Renoir, and complains:

It's a shame that the time of drawing from nature has passed forever.
No one needs this now—there are only "concepts" all around,
Abstractions, "installations" and other such talentlessness and frivolities.

Such is the mordant humor that braces Kabakov's melancholy, the gritty salt that cuts his sweetness.

I noted that the Kabakovs' doorbell at their Manhattan studio is marked by neither a name nor a number but a red blob. "Red Square!" Kabakov joked. Actually, the shape is round. A handy, human shape.

Portfolio

from The Palace of Projects

Ilya Kabakov

„НА ЗЕМЛЕ ЖИТЬ НЕЛЬЗЯ!"

Михаил Журавлев
г. Липецк

Общеизвестно, что экологическая ситуация на
поверхности нашей Земли складывается таким
образом, что от перенаселения, развития про-
мышленности и транспорта и общего отрав-
ления окружающей среды, жизнь большинства
населения не только в городах но и в так
называемых экологически чистых районах скоро
станет не только не безопасной но поп-
росту невозможной. В этих условиях рассе-
ление в двух, до этого не освоенных, зонах:
на больших океанских глубинах и высоко над
поверхностью Земли становится не только же-
лательным, но, по существу, и неизбежным. Ин-
тересно, что обе возможности напрямую оказываются
могут быть связаны друг с другом. Основная
трудность жизни в воздухе - преодоление гра-
витационного поля земли - может быть решена
самым неожиданным и тем не менее тех-
нически вполне осуществимым образом, о чем
рассказывается в предлагаемом проекте.
Уменьшение гравитационного поля земли вполне
возможно при создание огромных по размеру
энергетических колец переводящих массу (или
что тоже самое, гравитационный вектор) из направ-
ленности вверх в направление ему проти-
воположное. Подобные герметично изолирован-
ные кольца можно построить только в глу-
бине океана а внутри них естественно,
огромные зоны для проживания. Челове-
чество, тем самым „потерявшее в весе"
может свободно осваивать глубины воз-
душного океана, приспосабливаясь к нова-
открывшейся среде, пользуясь для средств су-
ществования или самой земной поверхностью
или устраивая жилища или „поля пропитания" в
самой воздушной среде, в ее чистом незагрязненном пространстве

IT IS IMPOSSIBLE TO LIVE ON THIS EARTH!

1. You need to build a special table, a rack from white metal pipes or metal poles with squared edges. There is no need to paint it, leave it in its natural metal form similar to aluminum.

2. Cover the table with glass (cf. sketch) and the 2 lower shelves from the bottom with glass as well. Enclose the back and the sides of the "table" with glass as well, leaving the open side turned towards the viewer. Everything taken together should resemble a medical cart for medicine in an operating room.

3. Build a model of a city with buildings, trees, etc. on the lower glass.

4. There are metal poles sticking out over the table. Tie them together with wire 4 mm in diameter or with metal pipes of the same diameter.

5. Pictures depicting flying people are arranged between two pieces of glass or plastic. Glue them on all sides with a paper glue ribbon and attach them to the wire with white clothespins.

6. Install three lights and illuminate the pictures and the model below.

Н. Либельс. Фотограф, г. Могилев.

„Уйти от себя"

Любому человеку знакомо чувство — одним в меньшей, другим в большей степени — тоски и усталости, доходящей иногда до отвращения, от самого себя: необъяснимое, но сильное желание как бы покинуть самого себя со всеми своими заботами и мыслями, делами, успешными или неудачными, безразлично; разорвать это кольцо, которое мы сами и другие называют „я" и выйти, уйти хотя бы на время по ту сторону своего существования, так хорошо знакомого и осточертевшего нам.

Некоторые бессознательно, чувствуя приближение такого состояния, стремятся поскорее сменить окружающую обстановку или занятия или устремляются в тесный дружеский или больший общественный круг, чтобы среди других голосов и разговоров не мог быть услышан голос, звучащий изнутри, или не звучал так громко. Другие привычно в таких случаях применяют всем известные средства — табак, вино, наркотики, — чтобы или заглушить так внезапно и с такой силой охватывающее вас состояние — но и первый и второй способ не дают спасения от мучительного чувства, не приводят к желанному освобождению, а лишь отодвигают его, загоняя душевную болезнь лишь еще глубже.

Наш проект предлагает, хотя он может показаться необычным, зато радикальный способ покидания „самого себя". Многим он покажется непосильным и даже страшным, но именно он, благодаря своей радикальности, способен быстро помочь освободиться от нас самих и по прошествии короткого времени вновь вернуться к себе уже обновленными и возрожденными к дальнейшему существованию.

Проект состоит в том, чтобы, выбрав небольшую площадку в городе (желательно не на особо людной улице), вы сняли с себя всю одежду и разложили ее, каждую часть в отдельности, на равном расстоянии одну от другой таким образом, чтобы все они образовали замкнутый круг с диаметром приблизительно в 2,5 метра. После этого, подстелив под себя небольшой коврик или доску, следует сесть на нее, приняв положение, указанное на рисунке. После пребывания в таком положении не менее 40–45 минут, следует повторить это в ближайшие два

TO ESCAPE FROM ONESELF

1. Here is a list of things which you should place on the floor in a circle with a diameter of 2.5 m:
    1. Underwear
    2. Tee-shirt
    3. Trousers
    4. Shirt
    5. Sweater
    6. Jacket
    7. Boots
    8. Coat
    9. Scarf
    10. Hat

All the things should be neatly folded and not just tossed around, the things should not be new but worn.

Р. Седов, Спортсмен, чемпион по бегу, г. Ворошилов.

ПРОЕКТ ОСТАВИТЬ ПАМЯТНИК О СЕБЕ

У каждого человека вполне естественное желание оставить по себе какой-нибудь памятник, и, конечно, чтобы он, по крайней мере, выполнил три условия: не мог бы исчезнуть за короткое время из-за непрочности материала, или из-за погодных или социальных катаклизмов; второе, — был в тоже время достаточно величественен и грандиозен, производил бы впечатление; и, конечно, третье условие: чтобы памятник носил отпечаток личности того, кому этот памятник поставлен, его неповторимой индивидуальности, а не только различным абстрактным идеям с которыми он соотносил себя в жизни.

Проект горного памятника, описанный ниже, удовлетворяет всем этим требованиям и добавляет еще одно свойство — его очень трудно повторить, он уникален в своем замысле и вне сомнения, может быть рассмотрен и принят личностью не только сознающей свою уникальность и исключительность но и желающую и после своей смерти остаться вдали от шума людского, замкнуться и вечно пребывать среди величественного и недоступного людям ландшафта.

В недоступной горной местности разыскивается высокая расщелина между скал с каменным широким плоским уступом внизу. С обеих ног того, кто хочет установить памятник, снимается гипсовый слепок до высоты голени, который и послужит моделью. После этого бригада взрывателей и каменотесов повторяет сначала в подошве скалы форму обеих ступней, пользуясь большим, но точным повторением модели, а затем в верхней части каменной расселины повторяет боковые части голени и задние части икр. После окончания этих скульптурных работ и полировки камня возникает эффект стоящей, и продавившей камень гигантской фигуры,

Нет никаких сомнений, что в скором времени об этом будут распространятся легенды и это место окажется целью паломничества, тем более желанным, чем оно более будет недоступным.

PROJECT TO LEAVE A MONUMENT OF ONESELF

1. Prepare a small box 42 × 50 × 10 cm with a quantity of wet plaster.

2. Place an irregular shape (sketch No. 1) with a thickness of 3 cm on the bottom of the box.

3. Step into the box with your bare feet (preferably men's feet, but women's are OK as well).

4. Begin to place the wet plaster, starting with the toes, not covering the foot on the top, and the back of the legs, not covering the calves from the front. The plaster should be poured in such a way that when it dries, you can easily remove your legs by stepping out of the plaster. The model is 52 cm high.

5. At the same time, make the side, external sides of the "sculpture" so that they resemble cliffs and precipices of a mountain mass.

6. Remove the finished model along with the board, and paint it like gray cliffs.

„Как изменить самого себя!“

Н. Соломаткин Шафер
г. Кишинев

Как сделать себя лучше, добрее, порядочней? Над этой задачей — как избавиться от большинства собственных недостатков, пороков, одним словом, как изменить себя в лучшую, нравственную сторону — бились не одно поколение моралистов, мыслителей, религиозных деятелей. Большинство видят единственную возможность в изменении самим человеком его внутреннего „я“, другие видят в неукоснительном следовании нравственным правилам, третьи в отказе от земных соблазнов и следовании по религиозному пути.

Какая из этих дорог правильна, став на нее можно добиться желанной цели. Не отвергая ни одну из них, наш проект предусматривает еще одну возможность. Она состоит в ежедневной процедуре, которая, несмотря на свою кажущуюся простоту, может оказаться чрезвычайно эффективной.

Нужно изготовить два крыла из белой тюлевой ткани, пользуясь тем чертежом который прилагается к проекту, а также кожанные ремни крепления для установки и фиксирования этих крыльев на спине. После этого, оставшись наедине в комнате (это условие достаточно важное, как для продуктивности предстоящего действия, так и для пресечения нежелательных реакций со стороны других членов семьи*) следует одеть на себя крылья, побыть в полном бездействии и молча 5-10 минут, после чего обратиться к своим обычным занятиям не выходя из комнаты. Через 2 часа вновь повторить начальную паузу. После 2-3 недель ежедневных процедур воздействие белых крыльев все с большей силой начнет проявлять себя

* По этому во время процедуры шторы на окнах должны быть спущены, двери занесены а крылья лучше всего

HOW CAN ONE CHANGE ONESELF?

1. Make two wings. First make two frames of wire and attach to them the wings made of white gauze. The frames should first be attached to two oval boards of plywood.

2. Make leather straps from belts which can attach to the shoulders, chest and waist. Attach the wings, which have already been attached to the boards to the straps.

3. For the exposition, both the wings and the straps should hang freely on the wall on a nail, as though it were an ordinary harness in a horse stable.

4. The length of each wing is 140 cm, the width from the center support is 40 cm.

from For the Time Being

Annie Dillard

I

June, 1923: The French paleontologist Teilhard de Chardin was traveling on muleback in the vastness beyond the Great Wall, west of Peking. He saw it from a distance: the Ordos, the inner Mongolian desert. He saw from the mule what he had seen often in Egypt years before, "the burnt stones of the desert and the sand of the dunes in the dusk."

The Ordos is a desert plateau 3,000 feet high, from which mountains rise. It spreads 35,000 square miles. The Great Wall separates the Ordos from the fertile lands to the east and south in Shansi and Shensi provinces.

He was forty-two years old, tall and narrow, fine-featured. He wore a big felt hat like a cowboy, and thick boots. Rough weather had cut lines on his face. He had carried stretchers during the Great War for a regiment of sharpshooters. His courage at the front—at Ypres, Arras and Verdun—won him several medals, which the surviving men of his regiment requested for him. One of his fellows recalled his "absolute contempt for danger" as he mounted parapets under fire. People shortened his name—Pierre Teilhard de Chardin—to Teilhard: "Tay-yard" in French.

His characteristic expression was simple and natural, according to one colleague, who also noted "his eyes, filled with intelligence and understanding." Another scientist described him as "a man of self-effacing and irresistible distinction, as simple in his gestures as in his manners . . . his smile never quite turned to laughter . . . anxious to welcome, but like a rock of marble." From the back of a jog-trotting mule, he could spot on stony ground a tiny rock that early man had chipped.

On some days in the Ordos he and his geologist colleague dug, excavated and sifted the ground. On other days they moved in caravan. They rode with two Mongolian soldiers—to fight bandits—and five so-called donkey boys. "On the third day," he wrote a friend, "we arrived at an immense steppe over which we traveled for more than six days without seeing much else but endless expanses of tall grasses." He passed the garnet and marble gorges of the Ula-Shan, "the old crystalline shelf of China."

July, 1923: Teilhard was one of the men who unpacked the expedition's three donkeys and ten mules for the night. Bandit raids had routed them from the steppes and forced them to enter the badlands. That night he and the others pitched their two white tents in the Ordos massif, within a circle of red earth cliffs. In one red cliff he found, by daylight, the fossil remains of extinct pachyderms from the Pliocene.

"The immense hazard and the immense blindness of the world," he wrote, "are only an illusion."

The scant rain that reaches the Ordos falls in thunderstorms. During a thunderstorm, the man wrote a letter. "Of this part of the journey, the crossing of the Arbous-Ula will remain in my memory as the finest stage. The innumerable strata of this savage mountain, a forward bastion of the Ula-Shan on the right bank of the Yellow River, bend gently into two long concentric folds which seem to unfurl over the eastern solitudes."

August, 1923: Once more they pitched their tents in the desert in a circle of cliffs. Here they camped for a month, in the southeast corner of the Ordos where the cliffs were gray, yellow and green. Here the great eroded loess hills met the sands a river laid—the river called Shara-Osso-Gol. And here they found the world's first evidence of pre-Neandertal man in China. *The man of the yellow earths*, Teilhard named him, for loess is a fine yellow dust. They found his traces in the Shara-Osso-Gol's twisted canyon.

First they found Neandertal tools ten meters down: scrapers, gravers, quartzite blades. Then they dug through 164 feet of barren sands before they found an ancient hearth where Paleolithic people cooked. People had lived in China long before Neandertal people lived in Europe. Their blackened hearth made a thin layer among cross-bedded dune sands and blue clays, near the river. No hominid bones were there, but some tools lay about, and the hearth was indisputable—the first human traces north of the Himalayas.

The people made these fires by this river about 450,000 years ago—before the last two ice ages. During their time, the Outer Mongolian plateau to the north continued its slow rise; it was blocking Indian Ocean monsoons. The northern plateau dried to dust and formed the Gobi Desert. The people would have seen dust clouds blow from the north, probably only a few big dust clouds every year. Such dust today! they must have thought. After the people vanished, the dust continued to blow down on their land; it laid loess deposits hundreds of feet deep. Almost 4,500 centuries passed, and in 1222 Genghis Khan and his hordes rode ponies over the loess plateau, over the hundreds of feet of loess deposits yellow and gray, over the fecund dust and the barren sand, and over the animal bones, the chipped blades and the hearth. Teilhard thought of this, of Genghis Khan and the ponies. "Much later," he wrote, "Genghis Khan crossed this plain in all the pride of his victories." At that time the Mongols made stirrups and horseshoes from wild sheep horns.

Teilhard found a twentieth-century Mongol family living in the Shara-Osso-Gol canyon. Their name was Wanschock. Wanschock and his five sons helped him excavate during the weeks he camped. They rode horses, kept goats and lived in a cave scooped out of a cliff in the loess. They taught their toddlers to ride by mounting them on sheep. "The Mongols wear long hair," Teilhard wrote, and they "never take off their boots, are never out of the saddle. The Mongol women look you straight in the eyes with a slightly scornful air, and ride like the men."

"Throughout my whole life," he wrote, "during every minute of it, the world has been gradually lighting up and blazing before my eyes until it has come to surround me, entirely lit up from within."

September, 1923: They rode back into Peking. The mules carried 5,600 pounds of fossils and rocks in 60 wood crates. The paleontologist Teilhard carried a notebook in which he had written, among other things, a morning prayer: "Be pleased yet once again to come down and breathe a soul into the newly formed, fragile film of matter with which this day the world is to be freshly clothed."

The realm of loose spirit never interested Teilhard. He did not believe in it. He never bought the view that the world was illusion and spirit alone was real. "There are only beings, everywhere," he had written in his notebook from a folding stool in the desert of the Ordos.

Matter he loved: people, landscapes, stones. Like most scientists, he was an Aristotelian, not a Platonist. When he was still in college he published articles on the Eocene in Egypt and the minerals of Jersey. In his twenties he discovered a new species of fish, and a new owl. His major contributions to science came later, when he dated Peking Man and revised the geology of all the Quaternary strata not only through China and Mongolia, but also through Java, India and Burma.

He spent twenty-three years of his adult life in China in rough conditions far from home. Why knock yourself out describing a dream?

"If I should lose all faith in God," he wrote, "I think that I should continue to believe invincibly in the world."

Teilhard had glimpsed the Gobi Desert from muleback on his 1923 Ordos expedition. It was the biggest desert on earth: 500,000 square miles of sandstorms and ravaged plateaus in what was then northern Mongolia. "As far as the eye could see around us, over the vast plain which had once been levelled by the Yellow River, waved the grass of the steppes." The solitudes moved him: the "wide torrential valleys where herds of gazelles could be seen, nose to wind, among the pebbles and the sparse grass . . . We were crossing the low steppes of San-Tao-Ho. The Mongolians are now no longer here . . . The season of the yellow winds is over."

The next morning he broke camp by the waters of the Shiling-Gol and moved towards Kalgan in the Gobi, an area science did not know. He found fossils. Two days later he was wielding a pick at the Dalai-Nor, a wet salt pan twenty-five miles long on the Mongolian steppe. He shook and spread his bedroll on a dune by the shore. Six oxcarts carried supplies and boxes of extinct Tertiary horse and rhino bones.

He resumed his teaching post in Paris the next year; in the next few years he lived again in China, undertook another Gobi expedition, returned to Paris, rode a mule on a geologic journey through the Mabla Massif in Ethiopia, and trekked for months digging bones and breaking rocks in both the Ordos and Manchuria.

In the field he wore a tough jacket and a wide-brimmed slouch hat. In one breast pocket he carried a breviary, and in the other a pack of Gauloises. "This man with the clear regard," a friend called him. He was long-boned, sharp-faced, faintly smiling when serious, and merry in company. When he laughed his face split into planes. All his life he parted his short hair on the side. His friends were mostly geologists, paleontologists, priests, explorers, educated Paris and New

York women, and archeologists. Among his friends were an odd trio: Julian Huxley, Henry Clay Frick and Paul Valéry.

He once called God *punctiform*. "It is precisely because he is so infinitely profound and punctiform that God is infinitely near." (Is it useful and wise to think of God as punctiform?)

Of the gospel miracles he wrote, "I feel obliged to admit that I believe not because of but in spite of the miracles."

Statistical probability describes the mechanism of evolution—chance operating on large numbers—so that, as Teilhard said, "at every moment it releases a given quantity of events that cause distress (failures, disintegrations, death)." That is, evolution's "every success is necessarily paid for by a large percentage of failures." In order to live at all, and to progress or even proceed, we pay "a mysterious tribute of tears, blood, and sin." It is hard to find a more inarguable explanation for the physical evil and the suffering we endure at chance from the material world.

"Even when we are exercising all our faculties of belief, Fortune will not necessarily turn out in the way we want but in the way it must."

Pierre Teilhard de Chardin was a Jesuit priest and writer as well as a paleontologist. The theology and cosmology that drove his thinking and writing are not his strongest legacy, any more than William Butler Yeats's theology and cosmology are. He wrote eighteen books. The unhappy prominence of his dull and crackpot *The Phenomenon of Man* thirty years ago, and the sometimes nutty enthusiasm of his admirers, some of them vague-brained New-Agers, have obscured his excellent *The Divine Milieu* and the short and magnificent literary essays "The Mass of the World" and "The Heart of Matter." The world rarely can or will distinguish art from mere opinion; pressed for his opinions, Teilhard produced them, and their peculiarly disagreeable lexicon, and the cranks they attracted in the U.S., possibly convinced some possessors of good minds to write him off without reading him.

He took theology courses for four years, and admitted that he did not find them *bien amusants*. He studied chemistry and physics in Cairo; at the Sorbonne he worked in botany and zoology as well as geology. His doctorate in geology described mammifers of the Lower Eocene in France.

He ran afoul of Roman authorities over his thinking. In the 1920s evolution was still a new current in thought, as the church reckoned, and it had not yet penetrated Rome's layers of brocade. The notion of biological evolution seemed to hash the old doctrine of original sin. After Teilhard lectured on evolution in Paris, the church in Rome gagged him. It forbade him to lecture and to publish anything but purely scientific articles. He complied. Of his eighteen books, the church permitted only one to see light in his lifetime, a short scientific monograph published in Peking. The cardinals were pleased to keep his person, also, tucked away. They exiled him to China, the second time for virtually the rest of his life. He was forty-three. Always longing for France, for his Paris teaching position, his Jesuit brothers, and friends, and always eager to settle for a life in the United States, he nevertheless discovered, gradually, that his vow of obedience required him to renounce the West for twenty-two years more.

Every year he applied to publish his work; every year Rome refused. Every year he applied to return to France. Every year Rome refused. At last Rome let him visit France when he was sixty-five; he had had a heart attack. Again, though, Rome prohibited his publishing. Offered a fine teaching post, he went to Rome in person to seek permission; Rome denied it. He traveled to the United States, to South America and to Africa, and he visited Paris to spread his ideas by talking. Even when he was seventy-three and dying of heart disease in New York, Rome forbade his publishing, lecturing and returning to France.

Why did he put up with it? One of his colleagues said he had "the impatience of a prophet." When did he show impatience? His colleagues and many of his friends urged him to quit the Jesuits. Only for a few weeks, however, did he consider leaving the order. To kick over the traces, he thought, would betray his Christianity. People would think he was straying from the church—perish the thought. His brother Jesuits defended him and his thinking. Leaving the order would mean, he decided, "the killing of everything I want to liberate, not destroy." The Catholic church, he wrote late in life, is still the best bet for an arch to God, for the transformation of man, and for making, in his view, evolution meaningful; it is "the only international organization that works."

He had dedicated his life wholeheartedly, again and again; consequently he did not complain. When he first learned that Rome banned publication of *The Divine Milieu*, he did, however, allow himself to write a friend in private that it was "a pity." The year before he died, while he was declaring in sincere letters that Rome was mankind's best hope, he also blew off steam, like many a cleric; he wrote a friend, "The sin of Rome is not to believe in a future . . . I know it because I have stifled for fifty years in this sub-human atmosphere." He apparently felt strongly both ways. Later Vatican II calmly endorsed most of his ideas.

"All that is really worthwhile is action," Teilhard wrote. "Personal success or personal satisfaction are not worth another thought."

II

"I feel no special assurance of the existence of Christ," Father Teilhard explained cheerfully at the end of a book in which he tracked his ideas. His evolving universe culminates in Christ symbolically ("Jesus must be loved as a world") and to a degree unpalatable. "As much as anyone, I imagine," he went on, "I walk in the shadows of faith"—that is, in doubt. Doubt and dedication often go hand in hand. And "faith," of course, is not assenting intellectually to a series of doctrinal propositions; it is living in conscious and rededicated relationship to God. Nevertheless, the temptation to profess creeds with uncrossed fingers is strong. Teilhard possessed, like many spiritual thinkers, a sort of anaerobic capacity to batten and thrive on paradox.

It was in 1928, when Teilhard was forty-seven, that his team found Peking Man. An archeologist, Pei Wen-chung, found a man's skull. Teilhard had unearthed the first tools and hearths in the Ordos, but here were the first bones. The skull from the cave near Peking caused a sensation; it was the first bit of ancient human bone unearthed in all Asia.

Time had stuffed Peking Man, and all his pomps and works, down a red fissure in a blue cave wall at Zhoukoudian. Fossils crammed the red fissure. The team called the skull's first owner Peking Man. His species was *Homo erectus*.

The team originally found the Zhoukoudian cave by questioning a big-city pharmacist. Many folk in China drink suspended fossil bone powders as elixirs—dragon's teeth; consequently paleontologists for two generations have checked Chinese pharmacies and asked, "Where did these bones come from?" Shopping for fossils, a specialist recognized an ancient human tooth. His inquiry led to the caves at Zhoukoudian—Dragon Bone Hill.

Teilhard hauled his camp cot from Peking, lived with Chinese villagers and directed the dig. Over years he sorted and eventually named the fissure's animal bones. He discovered bones from saber-toothed tigers, ostriches, horses, a large camel, buffalo, wild sheep, rhinos, hyenas and "a large and a small bear." Ultimately, and crucially, he was able to date Peking Man to the Pleistocene. He established the date by many methods, one of which was interesting: among the bits of debris under, around and above various layers of Peking Man's bones and tools were skulls of mole-rats, and pieces of skulls of mole-rats. He undertook his own study of the mole-rats' evolving skulls, dated them and so helped fix Peking Man's dates.

The team dug further into the immensities of the Zhoukoudian caves; for ten years they excavated, for eight months a year. Teilhard retrieved five more human skulls, twelve lower jaws, and scattered teeth. It was his major lifework.

During those ten years, squinting and laughing furrowed his face. His temples dipped as his narrow skull bones emerged. When he could not get Gauloises, he smoked Jobs. Daily he said the Divine Office—the liturgy, mostly psalms, that is the prayer of the Catholic church (and the Anglican Church). A British historian who knew him described his "kindly and ironic grace," his "sharp and yet benevolent refinement."

In all those years, he found no skeletons. When colleagues worldwide praised him for the discoveries, Teilhard spoke with modesty and exasperation: "Heads," he said, "practically nothing but heads." Paleontologists from all over the world are again—seventy years later, after several decades' chaos halted the work—finding hominid bones, and choppers and flakes, in the Zhoukoudian caves.

Peking Man and his people walked upright; with limbs like ours they made fire and stone tools. They ate mostly venison and hackberries. They hunted elephants, tigers and boars. They lived before water filled the Great Lakes and the Florida peninsula lifted from the sea, while camels and mastodons grazed in North America. They lived before two great ages when ice covered Scandinavia and Canada, and covered the British Isles, northern Germany and the northern United States; they lived before the Atlantic Ocean drowned eastern North America between glaciations. Their human species is extinct, like the Neandertals'.

Most paleontologists believed until recently that we—we humans in the form of *Homo erectus*—left Africa 90,000 years ago by walking up the Great Rift Valley, generation after generation, to the valley's end at the Sea of Galilee. Recent much older *erectus* finds in Java, China and the Republic of Georgia seem to show that our generations started leaving Africa about a million years earlier—unless humans arose in Asia. The new ancient dates jolt paleontologists, who one might expect would be accustomed to this sort of thing by now—this repeated knocking out the back wall, this eerie old light on the peopled landscape.

Whenever we made our move, we did not rush to Corfu like sensible people. Instead we carried our cupped fires into the lands we now call the Levant, and then seriatim into

China, Japan and Indonesia, whence we hopped islands clear to Australia. In Australia on a rock shelter we engraved animals twice as long ago as we painted cave walls in France. People—including *erectus*—plied Asian islands thousands of years before Europe saw any humans who could think of such a thing as a raft.

"However far back we look into the past," Teilhard said, "we see the waves of the multiple breaking into foam."

During the violence and famine when the Japanese invaded China during the Second World War, that first Peking-Man skull disappeared from the Chinese museum. Scientists suspect starving locals pulverized it and drank it. There is a plaster cast of this skull, as there is of every bit of bone and tooth—forty people's remains—that the team found by working the site for all those years. The plaster casts proved handy, as every single one of the Peking Man bones, crate after crate, disappeared in the war. When the Japanese invaded, scientists cached the crates with a U.S. Marine doctor who tried to carry them back as luggage. The Japanese caught him. Before he went to prison he was able to entrust the crates to European officials and Chinese friends. Four years later when the war ended he left prison; the crates had disappeared. Recent searches drew blanks.

The man of the red earths, Teilhard called Peking Man. And of Christianity he said: "We have had too much talk of sheep. I want to see the lions come out."

Teilhard, according to his biographer Robert Speaight, "was not very much bothered by 'who moved the stone.'"

"We are Christians," he wrote deadpan in a 1936 letter, "in a somewhat renovated manner." A modern abbot, Abbé Paul Grenet, quoted this in a 1966 biography, published by Eriksson, which describes Teilhard as always faithful to his calling and to the order of Jesuits.

"The great Neolithic proprietor," the paleontologist called him, the God of the old cosmos, who was not yet known as the soul of the world but as its omnipotent mage. This God caused everything that happened; history, then, was a fix. He called the idea that we suffer at the hands of an omnipotent God "fatal." It is fatal, that is, to the idea of God's omnipotence.

III

Early spring, 1930, Father Teilhard, wearing his clerical collar, was having afternoon tea in the Peking courtyard of his new friend, the American woman Lucile Swan. He sat erect and relaxed, on a bamboo chair at a rattan table laughing and talking. In the other bamboo chair Lucile Swan turned his way; she looked mightily amused. A headband held her short, curly hair from her firm and wide-boned face. She wore an open parka and pants; it was perhaps chilly for taking tea outdoors. Her small dog, white and brown, sat at her knee watching the merriment, all ears.

He was forty-nine; she was forty, a sculptor, divorced. It was over a year after the Peking Man discovery; he was living in a village near the Zhoukoudian cave and coming into Peking once a week. The two had met at a dinner party. They liked each other at once: "For the first time in years I felt young and full of hope again," she recalled. She had attended Episcopal boarding school and the Art Institute of Chicago. In Peking she made portrait sculptures in clay and bronze, and groups of semi-abstract figures; throughout her life she exhibited widely. Soon the two established a daily routine in Peking: they took a walk, had tea at five, and he returned across the city to the Jesuit house at six. Those first several years, they laughed a great deal—about, among many other things, the American comic "The Little King," which Lucile found in her *New Yorker*s and translated for him.

"Lucile was fine-featured, amply bosomed," a friend who joined them at tea recalled, "beloved by all who knew her. For she glowed with warmth and honest sentiment." And Father Teilhard was "a lean, patrician priest . . . the jagged aristocrat. He radiated outward, gravely, merrily, inquiringly.

And always with a delicate consideration for the other and no concern for self."

June, 1930: "Our blue tents are pitched at the edge of a fossil-bearing cliff looking out over the immense flat surface of Mongolia," he wrote. "We work in solitude." He knew he could not post this letter for several months, for he was tracing the wild bounds of Outer Mongolia. "Cut off from any correspondence, I feel that my Paris hopes are dormant." He was not yet writing letters to Lucile Swan. In the Gobi Desert—the "immense austere plains"—he lost a cigarette lighter. These things happen.

He had interrupted his Zhoukoudian caves excavation to join an American expedition—the 1930 Roy Chapman Andrews expedition, officially called the Central Asiatic Expedition of the American Museum of Natural History. Most of his past five years he had already spent traveling with mules to dig the great Gobi marches; the Roy Chapman Andrews expedition would take him even further afield. To fix Peking Man in context, he wanted to discover the geologic history of the Quaternary through all of Asia. And in fact, over the expedition's wild and crawling journey, which lasted most of a year, he found the evidence to link and date Chinese and Mongolian strata.

The American Andrews expedition was a step up for the monsieur accustomed to mules. They drove Dodge trucks. Strings of camels carried gas. Digging, they encountered between five and ten poisonous brown pit vipers every day. The vipers kept them alert, one team member reported; characteristically, Teilhard never mentioned them in his letters. He liked Roy Chapman Andrews, who made his name finding dinosaur eggs. "A wonderful talker," he described him, and a hunter who, when the team lacked food, drove off into the bright expanses and returned "with a couple of gazelles on the running boards." His own vitality still battened on apparent paradox. The man who said that his thirty months on the front in the war had made him "very mystical and very realistic" now wrote from his blue tent in Mongolia, "Rain, storms and dust and icy winds have only whipped up my blood and brought me rest." They called that place Wolf Camp, for the wolves and eagles hunted there.

"Purity does not lie in a separation from the universe, but in a deeper penetration of it," he wrote.

The next year he attached himself to a French expedition as its geologist. The 1931 *Croisière Jaune* expedition took nine months and crossed Asia to the Russian frontier. He doubled his knowledge of Asia. He went so far west he realized one day he was halfway from Peking to Paris. He and the other Frenchmen traveled by Citroën caterpillar across "great folds of impassable land." They breached what the paleontologist admired as the unending corrugations of the Gobi peneplain and the monumental formations of Upper Asia. They crossed a region where mountains rose 21,000 feet. The Silk Road's northern route took them west to the Pamir Mountains as far as Afghanistan. On the road, the others reported, the paleontologist often stopped his Citroën half-track, darted ahead into the waste and picked up a chipped green rock, a palaeolith or a knob of bone.

"This vast ocean-like expanse, furrowed by sharp ridges of rock, inhabited by gazelles, dotted with white and red lamaseries . . . I am obliged to understand it." He examined the juncture where the foot of "the huge ridge of the Celestial Mountains" plunged 600 feet below sea level into the Turfan Deep. The Turfan Deep, in turn, opened onto a "vast depression" in which the River Tarim lost itself "in the shifting basin of the Lop-Nor."

"I still, you see, don't know where life is taking me," he wrote his friend Max Begoüen. "I'm beginning to think that I shall always be like this and that death will find me still a wanderer." He was forty-eight. He was correct about his death.

Returning mid-winter, the team explored an immense section of the Gobi no one had mapped. The temperature stuck between −20 and −30 degrees C. They dared not let the caterpillars' engines stop. Twice a day they halted and stood, almost immobile in furs, by the mess-vehicle, and tried to drink boiling soup in tin mugs before it froze.

He wrote, "Till the very end of time, matter will always remain young, exuberant, sparkling, new-born for those who are willing."

By the time he was fifty, he said, he had awakened to the size of the earth and its lands. In only his first ten years there, he explored China at walking pace from the Pacific to the Pamir Mountains as far as Afghanistan, and from the Khingan Mountains northeast of Mongolia south to Vietnam. He had returned from the *Croisière Jaune* expedition, worked all spring in Peking and traveled throughout the fall. It was then, three years after he met her, that he began writing letters to the sculptor Lucile Swan with whom he had taken so much tea behind her red courtyard gate.

In his salutations "Lucile, dear friend" quickly became "Lucile, dear" and then "Dearest." She remained "Dearest" (sometimes he underlined it) for twenty-three years until he died. Their published correspondence—hundreds of letters apiece—knocks one out, for of course she loved him, and he loved her. "I am so full of you, Lucile.—How to thank you for what you are for me! . . . I think that I have crossed a critical point in my internal evolution, those past months,—with you.—" "My dream," he wrote her, "is to make you gloriously happy."

She translated his work. She molded for science a fleshed head of Peking Man. For her he sounded out his ideas. One idea he returned to drearily often was his commitment to his vows. He told her, "I do not belong to myself." In an essay he wrote, "Through woman and woman alone, man can escape from isolation"—but in right passion love will be, predictably, spiritual. "Joy and union," he wrote her, "are in a continuous common discovery. Is that not true, dearest?" He never broke any of his vows. (Both men and women who live under religious vows agree that while communal living irritates them most, obedience is by far the toughest vow, and not chastity as secular people imagine. Not a monk,

Teilhard had no trouble from twenty-four-hour communal living; obedience chafed him sorely; and he confided later that to maintain chastity he had, quite naturally, "been through some difficult passages.")

Lucile Swan wrote him, "It seems sometimes that I have to accept so *many* things." In her private journal she wrote, "Friendship is no doubt the highest form of love—and also very difficult." As the years passed, he lived in Peking and visited France; he traveled to South America, Burma, India, South Africa, Rhodesia and Java. They both lived in Peking, for the most part, for twenty-two years after they met, until in 1941 she moved to the United States. Missing him sometimes by a few days, she traveled in those years and in the following fourteen years to France, Rome, Ethiopia, Switzerland, Siam, London and India. In 1952, when he was seventy-one years old, he moved to New York City, where she was living and exhibiting. They met frequently; "We still disturb each other," he wrote her across town. Especially disturbing to her was his new and deep friendship with another woman—another American, a novelist.

Even three years later, after he had survived a heart attack, and after hundreds of their love letters had flown all over the world for decades, after hundreds of reunions and partings, and after hundreds of visits in New York, he wrote her that he hoped that "things" would "gradually settle emotionally." There was not much "gradually" left, as he died eleven days later. He was seventy-four. A snapshot of Lucile Swan outdoors in her sixties shows a magnificent beauty. A dog is looking at her face; the dog holds one end of a towel in its teeth, she holds the other in her hand; the dog is clearly waiting for her to do her part right. She lived ten years after he died.

"What is born between us is for ever: I know it," the man wrote her. One fervently hopes so. One hopes, too—at least this one does—that in heaven souls suffer fewer scruples, or, better yet, none at all.

David St. John

The Park

It was I think in a small town in Ohio

I taped to the wall above my office desk the postcard
Of Klimt's painting called *The Park*

An example of cliché so profuse it touched my heart

Consoling me each time I turned my glance to its
Storm of tiny moth-sized leaves shimmering over all but
the bottom

Ribbon of the canvas where the rows of the trunks individuate

The mass of the pulsing foliage above
A figure in a kimono or a robe so lush it too seems foliate

Stands apart from two other figures similarly dressed

But (the two) huddled closely together & moving off the sheer
Right edge of the canvas

& the solitary figure remains oddly hesitant & indistinct

& pensive although
Perhaps she is simply realizing that she does not wish to go

Where all of the others wish to go

Anne McCarty

Homage to H.D.

Hermione, Helen, Hilda, I have been,
my pencil picking from inside a weighted
statue, or tree, my skin stiffened, mated
to bark, bubbling, but I have peeled to green
to distinguish green from green, each shade and hue.
I was the cut Christmas tree, a hoop skirt,
the decorated, dragged ornament, girt
in crinoline, fire chewed fast; I knew
I should be burnt, a witch in Salem, *Run*
Hermione, run, before you solidify,
the frieze framing you, your coined profile
in gold—precious and owned, yes, you were one
full of flowers: asphodel, columbine,
and crocuses. You could not stop your mind.

Two Poems by Reginald Shepherd

Nights and Days of Nineteen-Something

for Marilyn Hacker

Midsummer with other men's lovers, fumbles
on a living room couch, significance asleep
upstairs: I come through the door, I come
through the door, I came and was

conquered by tensed thighs, taut buttocks.
Asses, asses, lust from lust, a must
of sweat on matted hair, a spill of semen
down my thigh. (Classicism revised, or

what shall we do with a drunken
torso, machine shop of body parts, some
of them functional. Pink petals
of an asshole opening under tongue,

pink cockhead swollen to bursting
purple balloon. It caught in the trees.)
Who am I to think that
I'm not always on my knees

taking in some stranger strayed too far
from what he wouldn't want
to work for, paying out the line
we've always used. *Hey, do you want*

a ride? I'm walking through a field
of safety glass without my shoes; it itches,
like a sneeze. (Say it, no things but in
ideas: desire, denial; define, defiler. Decide,

then choose for me. Mother may I
go down on this man?) The tuck
in my jeans itches afterward, salt
smudge under my knees. This

is for your body made out of words, more
the worse for wear if you were there, or
where I wanted me to be. *And where*
were you last night, young man? (Here's

a rumor someone passed along: I believed in
his present tense, wrapped in tinfoil and a tissue
paper ribbon, his cock worn to the right
and the several layers that kept me from it,

the shirt and several layers most of all.)
If you have many desires your life
will be interesting, a modernism of poverty
and stained sheets, twin bed he went to

with me, came up for air and other things.
It was never sex I wanted, the grand etcetera
with a paper towel to wipe it up. I wanted him
to talk to me about Rimbaud while

I sucked him off in the park, drunk
as any wooden boat and tasting of old cigarettes
and Bailey's Irish Cream, my juvenilia. *Don't talk*
with your mouth full. (In the clearing

at the bottom of the artificial hill, his two hands
covered every part of me until I couldn't be seen,
a darkness past the burnt-out lamppost.
We came up empty-handed. *You're so empty*

-headed sometimes.) I never wanted love
from him, his needs adhesive, clinging like

cold sweat, old sperm; I never wanted him
to ask anything of me but *suck my big*

white cock. I come home sticky with
his secrecies, wash them all
off. You were my justice, just my means
to sex itself, end justified by the mean

size of the American penis. Just keep going
that way. You'd like to sleep, you'd like to be
left alone for miles of near-misses, missteps, mirrors
in a public bathroom, all mistake

and brief apology. (My lakefront myths of you
all insufficient to the taste of come
lapping my tongue.) The jogging path
curves up into that dark place in the trees

just past the rusted totem pole. Let me
lick salt from white skin in the moon's first light
when it lies brightest: argent, ardent, concrete
and utter falsehood. Comely, my comeuppance,

comfort me: come to mind at any time,
come again for me. Take me to the boy.

Reasons for Living

I was walking with the backward
river, sluggish water dialects
spell out spilled lakefront's
tumbledown babble of dressed
stones, nervous dogs and "no
swimming" pictographs: the land
washes ashore with under

clinging to it, undermining
crumble, halted fall. We pick our way
to level rock, watch out for oblique
angle slabs, it's so hot
we take off our pants, we lie down
and are grass, that green
and spore-filled, well-adapted
to be carried on the wind.

Mold-colored water dulled
as with use (pastel, must-
muddled nephrite, more common
than true jade, less highly prized,
its luster oily rather than vitreous,
a scum spilled across perspective)
with a turquoise line to build horizon
out of: prehnite, andradite,
alkali tourmaline, a seam of
semi-precious chrysoprase: anything
but true emerald, a grass-green beryl,
smaragds, prized for medicinal
virtues: uvarovite even rarer
among garnets, its crystals typically
too small to cut.

A broken landscape (man-made)
says to its place, "I don't
remember you," unphrased,
grooved by the gaze, chiseled
into being unseen, a glancing
blow: incursions of the geometric
(cement no place to rest your head),
naked economy, awkward skin
on green towels. And then a stirring
at the other side of when,

complicit blood flows back
into the stem, in retrospect
unfinished: we stand up
erect as grass, xylem, parenchyma,
epidermis, leaf blade and sheath.

Christopher Patton

The Death of Pliny the Elder

To man alone of all animated beings has it been given to grieve. Man is the only being prey to ambition, to avarice, to an immoderate desire of life, to superstition—he is the only one that troubles himself about his burial, and even what is to become of him after death.

—Pliny

Graft

I

An eye is opened
in a tree
by paring away the bark,
and a second
twig slipped in. Sap
seeps from the slit, a well-shaped
tear that hardens. The scion mends
on minerals
leached from mountain rubble by a running stream.

II

Gold from shafts in hills
will gild the palm
of a god
or a tedious official.
Rivers redirected
fifty leagues by aqueduct
rinse the ore in channels, and fill
our jewel boxes
with rings of a pure ill-gotten yellow.

III

A woman may wear
gold along
her arms, and rivers of gold
meander
down her sides, and learn
new ways to flow each time she turns
and sighs on a couch. Waking far
from her riches
in a frightening dream, she gasps like a wasp

IV

sinking stingless
in amber.
She wakes to wealth. The amber rubbed between
her fingers
to vivifying heat
gathers dried leaves and chaff—carved
into a tiny human effigy,
I've known it to
sell for more than living men in vigorous health.

Leaf

In that poor man's field,
sun spurs the dirt
to fecundity: a shoot
nudges aside a sod and unfurls a weak flag.
Caesar sees. Tiberius
sets dirt beds in frames on wheels
and chases the sun
with his tomatoes: they darken
with a warm and spreading red.
He thinks they blush at his command.

Scion: living portion of a plant joined to a trunk by grafting.

Give The Paris Review!

NO POSTAGE
NECESSARY
IF MAILED
IN THE
UNITED STATES

BUSINESS REPLY MAIL

FIRST-CLASS MAIL PERMIT NO. 3119 FLUSHING, NY

POSTAGE WILL BE PAID BY ADDRESSEE

THE PARIS REVIEW
45-39 171 PL
FLUSHING NY 11358-9892

Such food needs no fire
other than the fire
that formed invisibly
a seed. It flares in the apple rotting on a twig
out of reach, in the pear
we slice in half and stare
into, even in the useless
windfalls—spilt, bruised, skin-split,
their flesh will fold in defeat
but the seed survive. It flares in fabled men who, living

to taste the apples
in the Garden
of Hesperides,
turned godly. I close the manuals. In a ritual
way, I store sorb apples in clay
pots with broken floors to bury
upside-down, two feet
deep in a sunny spot. He does not know the soil's
benediction, who hunts
painted birds beyond the river Phasis.
Inestimably precious,
they are dangled from heaven as playthings.

Sheaf

I

The papyrus root
lies obliquely
in Nile mud: burns in mud
huts on the riverbank. Natives chew the stalk for juice
or make clothes
from it, rough mats, ropes,
sails for a funereal barge. Ten cubits tall,
triangular, tapering
gracefully upward, the stalk

is slit with needles
to the thinnest leaves:
substanceless surfaces.
Built up on a table moistened with Nile water,
crosswise in layers,
the paper
descends with seraphic grace to the muddy world
and lives a life among us
though not, bearing our words, of us.

II

A nightingale pours
forth song, grave,
sharp notes broken or
prolonged from a branch, quavering with a selfless
joy. Two chicks
beside him cock
their heads, strive to repeat what they hear,
and learn, by nature, what we
earn by art and squander.

With your finger
trace the hand
of Virgil, who traced
the journeys of our founder; the hand of Cicero
who civilized the Forum.
Before the fire
I strive to rewrite what they wrote. What use?
The Caliph will conquer, and these books
heat the baths of the city

There is a story, likely apocryphal, that when the Muslims conquered Alexandria in 642 A.D., the caliph Omar decreed that the books would "heat the baths of the city for six months."

Alexandria.
There the Great
discovered paper,
and built an hourglass spit of land that with years of silt
now holds a low salt sea
from the sea
without. On that edge, his library
receives our memory,
seawrack on a weak and brackish wave.

Wine

My tremulous
hands unable
to hold the over-
flowing vessel.
Within its swirling forms
a formal banquet room—
I see red veins under the cheeks of Caesar;

on that map
the weak, thin wine of empire
spreads, as his wife
takes her bath
for hours, in the milk of half a thousand asses.
Serving unspeakable thirst,
the hand on the nipple or
the finger at the rim
begs for an end to nothing, but nothing holds.

Hale

As diamond
struck on an anvil
splits the anvil,

NOTE: Pliny's epilepsy is my invention.

Death will divide me from you
my new one. Hovering
invisibly,
crystalline, a breath frozen round me,
he sends quakes through the clay within me.

Wracked with seizures
I eat the lights of a hare
with myrrh, or
drink horse piss in smithy water
fresh from a forge whose weapons
have won a day's
steady position.

Once, in the lost
Colossus of the Sun
at Rhodes,
I poked my head into the limbs
where they had shattered.
The sunlight's shafts
and intangible columns
all day made animate the dust.

Lull

I

Because the lion loves
the lamb, the lamb
dies. The eagle eats its eyes,
and green brown-maned grasses grow through the jaws.
Seeing ourselves
without cover, hide,
or scale, or the down granted a lion cub, a lamb,

"Lull" is based in part on a letter from Pliny the Younger to his friend Tacitus, the historian.

we've made you children swaddling clothes of the beasts
    we catch in woven
    hunting nets. And not by malice but love
  skewed is your soul
  forged into our toils.

  When scythes have slit the wheat,
the flax stalks are cut,
and for the coats to steep
  and loosen, are plunged in a vat and sunk with weights;
    hung and turned head downward
    in the sun, they dry. Laid
out then on stones, like infant kings to be found,
the worst are combed with iron hatchels for lamp wicks,
    the best carefully
    worked into nets so fine, one man can carry
  enough to harvest
  an entire forest.

II

  We have formed a cloth
incombustible,
a "live linen" woven
  of asbestos. Around a tree trunk, it silences
    the axeblow. And once a napkin
    made of the stuff, stained
with spreading archipelagos of wine,
was thrown into the banquet's blaze, and we, amazed,
    ceased a drunken song
    when after some seconds it rose on tongs
  more white and pure
  than thought could endure.

III

  A monarch's corpse will wear
a shroud of live linen

to keep his ashes
apart from the ashes of the pyre. Though there are places
which are always burning,
in 79, admiring,
admiral of the fleet at Misenum,
I first thought the plume rising from Vesuvius
harmless, a pine headed
heavenward. When soldiers at the foot sent for help
my light, steady
vessel was readied—

but the sea roiled with debris
at Retina, we
could not land. "Fortune
favors the brave," I said, "conduct me to Pomponianus."
At Stabiae, across the bay
I found my friend afraid.
To make calm, I bathed and dined with him, then dozed
as the courtyard filled with cinders and pumice stones.
The building, rocking, woke me.
We walked to the ships, protecting our heads
with pillows tied on.
Stones rained and ruined.

IV

The lion bites the dirt
when about to die,
and weeps. But he's kingly
investigating rolling wheels on an empty chariot
with vultures overhead; child, he fears
but does not flee the flame
brightening in his pelt. As his gaze rules
grasses without deceit, and lets no glance inward
remain oblique,
so did I, carrying a torch into that smoke,
form a third eye
and consent to die.

On a sea too boisterous
to set out upon,
the ships rose and keeled.
We boarded to wait. I lay down on a sail and asked Marcus
for water. When the air fumed
with sulphur (the smoke plume
that had seemed a pine tree was falling on us)
I asked for more. When the others had fled
through the brown and yellow
air, I tried to rise, and fell. I felt
come upon me
an uncommon calm.

The Vine Maple

becomes an image
of what it fears: beneath the conifers,
leaves arrayed in parallel sun-angling planes that flare
gold in such deep shade or
brandish firefighter reds as fires rage
in fall on open slopes; spreads through regions moist to
wet, clear-
cuts often, and lava flows; wants either courage

or rain. Sites on fire
are later favored by Douglas fir, from whose needles
the gold-nubbed chanterelles poke with their
undulating
gills; beneath whose flutings
of ridged, rough, mud-brown bark, the wood, admired
by rained-on Coast Salish as fine fuel even as it threw
troublesome sparks, seeped a pitch that soothed wounds,
and made strong spears,

The Coast Salish are the North Americans indigenous to southwest British Columbia. The Déné are native to northwest Canada and the Alaskan interior.

salmon weirs and fire
tongs. On every cone, thin green bracts poke out
from under the scales in three-forked slips—feet and tails
of hiding mice who've failed
in some small quest. (Bees nearby, full of fear,
hoard from black cottonwoods a sweet balsamic anti-
infectant resin: that mouse who enters the hive will mire,

die, and not rot). The Great
Spirit gave to the Salish redcedar
to honor that man always helping others. Tree
of Life with scale-like leaves
overlapping in a woman's long plait—
the bark made clothes, the wood became their dugout canoes
and bailers, combs, fishing floats, cradles, coffins, spirit

whistles and berry-
drying racks. Above, below the cedar
whose kindness is such that a stranger needing strength
need only stand beneath
with her back to the trunk, my landlady,
a lawyer half-Déné, from the porch pours rainwater out
of our old beer bottles. It is enough to see clearly.

These poems are spoken by the Roman scholar Pliny the Elder (23-79 A.D.) to his nephew Pliny the Younger, whom he adopted as his son in 73 A.D. Phrases from his work, sometimes adulterated, are used liberally through the first six poems.

Touch

Robert Coover

They meet, without touching, at the edge of two stories, his unfolding, hers under revision, or perhaps hers rising, his falling, brushing past one another with no more contact than that made by two empty coats in a restaurant cloakroom, say, one being checked in as the other is returned to its owner, who leaves, arm entering a sleeve, without remark, though not without a glance at the other, a glance returned, the first perhaps of their touches, speaking loosely, but across a dim entryway and nothing in it, more like a casual jostle than a touch, the sort of meaningless contact of eye or body parts one might endure in the elevator or a subway car, or else in a crowded theater lobby, where such a glance or heedless bump might lead to conversation, or at least an apology or an introduction—Haven't we met?—whereupon what was once a glance steadies to momentary scrutiny and the face feels stroked by something not unlike light, but softer than that, and then hands clasp briefly, though in the formal manner, stiff as sticks and as if thickly gloved, and further encounters are arranged, a return to the theater perhaps, why not: Dinner before?

And thus arises the prospect, however fleeting, furtive even, of something more than bump or jostle, as when two knees meet beneath the table, thighs spread toward one another in theater seats or in a taxi, or knuckles graze knuckles while donning coats or receiving drinks at intermission, she having bought this round perhaps, he telling her as he lifts his glass to her about a workplace scandal (the boss again!) or else about his grandmother: Careful, she always used to say, you can't unscramble an egg. Oh yes, she nods and smiles: I know. Remarks then—whether about politics or books or travel, dreams or food—feel not unlike little hugs or nudges, friendly pats upon the bottom, busses on the cheeks, though actually none of these occur, not yet, nothing more than a caressing gaze, a leaning toward, a suggestive gesture interrupted—his close whisper in the sculpture gallery, her dreamy smile at taxi's door—and in that tender space before touch resolves to touch: the smell of breath and hair and skin, each fragrance bearing a history of sorts, but one intangible and so still obscure.

Just so, obscurely, intangibly, so many of their stories have begun and ended, her body gloving itself as did her hands when first they met, his hands too easily sunk in pockets, or untimely occupied with doors or drinks—but then, quite unexpectedly, as when a sentence interrupts itself, or a new paragraph abruptly breaks upon the page, their hands spring free of old restraints and arc toward one another as antennae might, alert and curious, almost quivering before they touch, as touch they must (she cannot stop this, he cannot) and cover one another (his cover hers), stroke palms (hers his) and wrists, this in a city park or a hotel bar or a movie lobby maybe, both of them reeling from the marvel of it, and then, wherever they are, doesn't matter, lips find lips and tongues like facial fingers tongues, their hands now racing past the other's to search out flesh till now unseen, all but unimagined, shirttails ripping out like unbound pages from belted trousers, skirts hiked or fallen, undergarments stripped away and tossed into the intersection or the next row of seats, or onto the neighboring tables, spilling wine and soup.

Then, for a moment, thus exposed (they'll pay for this), they pause, blinking at one another in pure amaze, all rest erased from sight, first caress now pressed to tender clasp, to squeeze, to stroke and grasp and feverish embrace (the pause is past), their hands clutching not at flesh but at those deeper places flesh conceals, their mouths voraciously searching for other mouths below, both astonished that fingertip to tip should lead to this. What's happening—?! she gasps, he gasps, as their fingers probe past all last resistance: here a hand strives through muscle to grab at bone and sinew, pushing into the other's limb as might an arm slip into sleeve, and there another glides behind a breast to stroke gland and rib and ride the bellows of the wildly heaving lungs. A tongue, finding a navel or perhaps a scar (on an elbow, say, a thigh, under the chin), dives in, dragging the head and all else with it, the other plunging into ear or armpit, the two of them thus, at once, absorbing all and being all absorbed. Membranes dissolve, ligaments are lashed by eyelids and dampened by the overflow of lachrymal canals (what bliss!—if it's not terror), bones knock on bones, and blood vessels, nerves and entrails twine like clambering vines, all zones erogenous, and none. Darling, he whispers to her storied heart or else her spleen or pineal gland (he's somewhat lost in here), I almost cannot breathe! I know, she tells his bladder or perhaps one cranial lobe or other, causing his articulations (what was his name?) to twitch and jostle her in all her parts, I would get out of this, but as I'm both out and in I cannot think what out can mean!

They try to disengage—they've gone too far!—and, there, fingers reach out between a set of toes, or genitals or mouths appear behind the knees or nape, while here a brow is furrowed by another brow; but it's no use, their minds, awash with another's juices, and with their own, so puddled all together now, cannot so much as reason up a phrase to express their plight, much less escape it, if plight it is and not some terrible transfiguration of delight. Eyes blink through nostrils at the sudden hostile glare about and as suddenly recoil, and then the nostrils, too, withdraw, and if a hand, an arm, emerges from an anus, that arm thrusts forth only to the elbow that it might double back to burrow in again at sacrum's hollow. Their senses all are seized. They cannot see without for all they see within, a sight more akin to taste or smell, these senses in turn possessed by visions, or so it feels to them if feeling can be told from being felt. And so all boundaries dissolve and even of the self, as surfaces are by other surfaces consumed, all edges gone, skin less integument than vestibule, their limbs on view now eight, now none, their passions and their dreams (of spell-breaking intermission buzzers, say, or waiters bringing bills) as raveled as their organs and their bird's-nest veins.

This state of things cannot go on, yet cannot not go on, their stories, story, fused to one, spun out anew from knotted viscera and running on without their leave, even their imagined dialogues of release (Thank you, I loved the show. Yes, it's been quite entertaining. Or were we having supper? I hope I've not left anything behind. This stringy bit perhaps is yours? Oh, sorry, I hardly know what to say, I feel so out of joint! I know—here, let me help. Thank you, you've been so—no, no! *Don't touch*—!) imagined whole by this compounded creature that they've become yet cannot long remain, the world having no place for tormented soup-spilling two-headed and -hearted eight-limbed things, even if not always all at once on view. It—they—'ll be ripped clean apart, or not so clean, left at loose ends, so to speak, what raw portion attaching to each as may, but meanwhile, hashed up together still, they pitch and tumble through a world now less a world to them than mere veiled medium for their convulsions, wistfully storying as they go their implausible escape and dreaming of those bygone tranquil days of obscure bump and jostle . . .

Have you seen my, you know—the part that goes in here—?

Could that be what's up by dose?
No, that's my foot, I think, or yours.
Aha. Is this a parable or what?
A lobby, I believe. Or else a ballpark.
Oh my god, I feared as much. Do you have the coat checks?
Listen, who we are—
I know, *I know!* And what about this wriggly thing?
Just leave it on the plate . . .

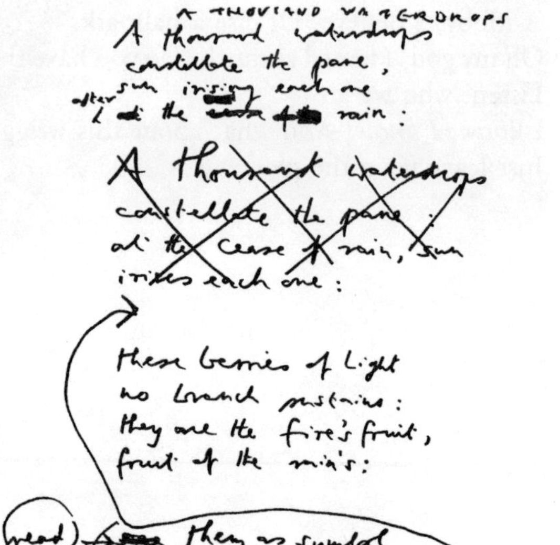

A manuscript page for the poem "A Thousand Waterdrops."

© Joachim Utz

Charles Tomlinson

The Art of Poetry LXXVIII

This interview was conducted through a series of letters, followed by a full afternoon of conversation in July 1998, at the Tomlinson house in Gloucestershire—its quaint and typically English address, Brook Cottage, Ozleworth Bottom, Wotton-under-Edge. The Tomlinsons have lived at Ozleworth since 1958. Originally, they bought one half of the cottage, then—three years later—the other, breaking through a wall to expand their space. With its stone walls, slate roof, low-beamed ceilings and casement windows, the house fits anyone's postcard or dream image of idiomatic English architecture. Outside, a border garden surrounds the cottage; on a moist midsummer day it was bursting with hollyhocks, flowering mint, buddleia, deep purple poppies and (of course) roses.

The interior of the cottage reflects simultaneously the Tomlinsons' unshakable Englishness and their lifetime of international travel and living abroad. Staffordshire figurines stand on bookcase and mantel; Victorian commemorative china and faience from Quimper decorate the walls, along with prints by Hiroshige and Piranesi. A beautiful nineteenth-century parlor piano with intricate carving stands across from the stereo. Brightly colored Indian fabrics, Mexican candelabras and Native American artifacts add still more generous accents.

The poet—tall, rail thin, courtly—wears an impressive jet ring, set in silver and extending to the knuckle; it is a memento of travels in, and fondness for, the American Southwest. Tomlinson met his wife, Brenda, in their native Stoke on Trent when he was sixteen and she fifteen. She was so blond that he thought she must have come from the large immigrant Czech community that had settled in Stoke during the 1930s. She was, in fact, the postman's daughter.

Charles Tomlinson's first "pamphlet of verse," entitled Relations and Contraries *was published in 1951. In his 1985* Collected Poems *he chose to include only a single poem from the early work, so his first "authentic" book was* The Necklace *(1955). In* Seeing Is Believing *(1958) Tomlinson achieved his characteristic voice and subject matter: the poetry since then has been marked by a painterly attention to landscape and to place in general, by an objective rendering of scenes and characters, and above all by a reluctance to indulge in confessional, narcissistic self-displays of emotion or melodrama. Since the* Collected Poems, *four elegant shorter volumes have appeared, the latest of which is called* Jubilation *(1995), which puns on the Spanish* jubilación, *the word for retirement.*

Having retired in 1992 from a long teaching career at the University of Bristol, Charles Tomlinson was prepared to de-

vote himself full-time to reading, writing and translating, with occasional travels and lecturing. In 1997 a botched routine cataract operation deprived him of sight in his left eye. In the following months the poet suffered an understandable (and by his own admission, uncharacteristic) depression. Brenda, his wife of fifty years, pulled him through with a combination of attentive care, cheerfulness and reading aloud. The Tomlinsons have made such recitations a standard part of their life together, and the poet said that during his convalescence War and Peace *and all of Jane Austen brought him around. "Why have books on tape, when I have Brenda?" he asked.*

INTERVIEWER

In your poem "Jubilación" you write about rejoicing in retirement. Obviously, the ordeal with your sight was unanticipated: how has it affected your retirement?

CHARLES TOMLINSON

You begin with the very episode I'm trying to put behind me, the failure of a cataract operation. A good place to begin in some ways, then we can put it behind us both. Although the loss of central vision in my left eye came as a great shock, I've managed to finish a new book called *The Vineyard Above the Sea*. The title poem is partly a response to Paul Valéry's "Le Cimetière Marin," but also a continuation of my many poems of gratitude to Italy. In addition to that, I've gone on to write a surprising number of things drawn from the Cotswold area in which I've long lived and to which I've now retired. So it's really business as usual.

INTERVIEWER

Have you come to rely more on your ears than your eyes at this point?

TOMLINSON

I still gather nourishment from sources that have been there for a long time. I've always counted on the ear as well as the eye—what poet doesn't? So whatever adjustments have been taking place, or may take place, there's no overnight somatic transformation to report: I continue to look with the right eye, though I no longer experience the easy panoramic sweep with which I once read a landscape, and the same is true of reading a book. I'm painfully aware of that. But translating painful awareness directly into verse has never been my way. One thing I will confess—the period of this unanticipated injury has required much coming to terms with. I think I'm through the first phase. Despair is no longer perpetually at my elbow. The anger I felt at first (perfectly irrational) with fate or whatever has slackened, though not completely disappeared. I have so many friends, and that awareness has sustained me and moved me away from self-involvement. And I have my wife. Indeed, before the ghastly surgery took place, I wrote for her and for them the little poem that concludes my *Selected*—the New Directions volume of last year—and that poem places eye and ear in some kind of perspective. It's called "A Backward Glance":

Searching my verse, to read what I'd once said,
It was the names on names of friends I read
And yours in every book, that made me see
How love and friendship nurture poetry.

INTERVIEWER

Although you claimed to look forward to retirement, it would seem that a backward glance would also be inevitable. Your career has gone on for almost fifty years. How would you characterize its progress? Could you begin with your education, first at school and then at university? How did you prepare to become a poet?

TOMLINSON

When I got to university I was deeply disappointed. I realized rather quickly that the teaching from my tutor at Cambridge was inferior to the stimulus I had received at school. You need two good teachers in any school, which is what we had, to get through the message of civilization—the role schools are there to fulfill. I owe everything to my two good teachers: Gerhardt Kuttner (soon to be anglicized as Gerard Cutner), a German Jew and a refugee from Hitler, who taught us German; and a Scot, Cecil Scrimgeour, who taught us French and who was much influenced by the Quakers and yet admired the civilization of Louis XIV's France. When I told a colleague in the French department at the University of Bristol a few years ago that at school we read Racine, Corneille, Molière and worked our way in considerable detail through an anthology containing Hugo, Baudelaire, Gautier and Verlaine, he said, "We don't expect that kind of thing nowadays." I felt his tone meant he thought I was exaggerating. What I didn't tell him was that this anthology contained a thorough account of French versification and that we'd also done a Balzac novel. Our German wasn't as concentratedly taught as that, but to have a grounding in Schiller, Heine, Kleist and Carossa was no mean beginning, and to have someone who could explain to us Kant's categorical imperative, give us a rapid outline of Nietzsche, introduce one to the work of Rilke, describe the way Thomas Mann pared an apple with surgical precision—well, all that was opening a way beyond the black industrial town where I was born into a sense of Europe itself.

INTERVIEWER

So reading took you from the provinces into a more cosmopolitan, or international frame of mind?

TOMLINSON

It was that sense of belonging to Europe, which took root early in my imagination. When our French teacher, as background to Racine, gave us a course on tragic drama, reaching back to the Greeks, and actually quoted from Aristotle's *Poetics*, my heart stood still. He explained all the Greek terms like *peripeteia* and *anagnorisis* to us. So when I saw Puccini's *La Bohème* (my very first opera) at the local theater, I noted how many of these terms applied to the Puccini and, back at school, told him of this. "Yes," he said, "but rather cheaply embodied." My feelings were a little dashed. I still think he was somewhat hard on Puccini, but the salutary challenge introduced me to the notion of critical standards, and the realization that terminology in the abstract couldn't really help you with the question of quality. A good early warning about the futility of theory.

INTERVIEWER

How about life at Cambridge?

TOMLINSON

My final year at Cambridge was a compensation for my first. I acquired a new supervisor, a young man just returned from service at sea, and this was Donald Davie. We went on to educate each other and ultimately to criticize each other's verse. This was the beginning of a fifty-year friendship, ending only with Donald's recent death. Without his introduction and approval of my first real collection, *The Necklace*, I should not have found my way into print. His thinking about poetic syntax in *Articulate Energy* clarified my own enormously and in many ways prepared me to write my first full-scale book of poems, *Seeing Is Believing*. This book, with the help of another friend, Hugh Kenner, who like Donald saw and believed, found a publisher in New York, beginning what was to be a long and fruitful relationship with America. The youthful European needed that. There *was* a new world. Henry James complained that it had no ruins. But he had never been to the deserts of the Southwest and seen the cliff dwellings of the Canyon de Chelly or the remains of Quarai and those in Chaco Canyon. All that, alongside modern America, was part of my continuing education—something Cambridge had failed to prepare me for.

INTERVIEWER

Although characteristically British in style and temperament, you have been unusual in your affection for America—

its landscape, people and art. How did this come about? With what provocation?

TOMLINSON

You're absolutely right. When I first went to America, it was the place you didn't go to. When I got back, people said, "Glad to be home, I imagine." My resolute reply was always, "Not particularly." How did it happen, my being drawn to America? All bits and pieces, to begin with. A monochrome reproduction of a Georgia O'Keeffe in a book that was a twenty-first birthday present (we were to meet her in New Mexico), a fascination with the poetry of Stevens and of Marianne Moore that was later to extend itself to Williams, thanks to the insistence—which I first of all resisted—of Gael Turnbull. Gael was one of those people American poets had reason to be grateful to. He spoke up for Williams, and from Migrant Books in Worcester he distributed Charles Olson, Robert Creeley, William Bronk, Allen Ginsberg. In his review, *Migrant*, there were French Canadians and there was Ed Dorn.

INTERVIEWER

Did this Americaphilia (if I may coin the term) affect your status as a fledgling poet back in Britain?

TOMLINSON

Having come under the influence of Stevens fairly early, I didn't find it easy to publish my poems in England, so I started sending them to *Poetry* magazine. Henry Rago, the editor then, was a great editor. Much to my amazement, I was awarded a number of prizes by *Poetry* (something that could not have happened here and hasn't since). Then Hugh Kenner persuaded his own publisher, McDowell, Obolensky, to take on *Seeing Is Believing*, a book just about everyone had refused in England. After its publication Henry wrote to ask if I was interested in being considered for one of the scholarships from the Institute of International Education, which aimed to facilitate travel in the States for young European writers. So off we went, Brenda, myself and our young daughter, and the greatest adventure of our life began. And great friendships began too. I think especially of those with James Laughlin and with Fred Morgan, who in *The Hudson Review* had been one of my first publishers along with *Poetry*.

INTERVIEWER

In addition to American poets, you came to know all sorts of other people, and to visit landscapes that even Americans in the fifties were rather unadventurous about seeing. What about the painters?

TOMLINSON

As I mentioned, my sense of America cohered out of many fragments, among them that tiny reproduction of a Georgia O'Keeffe, utterly unknown here at the time. I came to America at a period when the New York School had shifted attention from Paris to that city. For me, it was one of those periods of rapid assimilation—Jackson Pollock, Willem de Kooning, Arshile Gorky, particularly Gorky. But then I wanted to know more about what came before and gradually, or rather in quick leaps during the years, I managed to acquaint myself with the whole long story, going back to the Hudson River landscapes of Frederic Church and other nineteenth-century painters. I became a friend of the great collector Seymour Adelman, largely because he heard me read a poem on Thomas Eakins. He came up to me after the reading and said: "Would you like to see some of Eakins's photographs?" Ask and it shall be given! I asked a Sante Fe friend of Georgia O'Keeffe how I could get to see so reclusive a person. That, too, was arranged, and one morning—we were living in Albuquerque at the time—a telegram arrived from Abiquiu with an invitation to lunch. When I wrote up the visit many years later and it appeared in *The Hudson Review*—O'Keeffe was in her nineties by this time—another telegram and another invitation. She'd actually read the article. So America meant places and art, and it also meant people.

INTERVIEWER

You have made part of your mark throughout your career as a translator. You began with Italian poetry; a few years ago I heard you lecture on Dryden. Obviously you had languages when at school; students today (at least in the States) generally do not. How did you make this particular turn?

TOMLINSON

What luck I had to be educated by the two teachers I've already told you about. Of course, we learned Latin, too, and although it wasn't brilliantly taught, the form and logic of the language helped reinforce the lessons of French and German. This meant when I got a job in Italy I could pick up the language with relative ease. When I'd returned to England and later got a job at the University of Bristol, I met a fellow teacher, Henry Gifford, who knew both Russian and Spanish. He somehow conveyed enough Russian to me to permit me to collaborate with him on a little book, *Versions from Tyutchev*. After which he said, "Why don't we do some Antonio Machado?" "But I don't know Spanish . . ." The same persuasiveness as before, with incredibly detailed "transparencies," as Henry called them—literal translations plus notes line by line beneath the originals. The closeness of Spanish to Italian also helped me here. Eventually I realized that I really must learn Spanish, and my friendship with Octavio Paz gave me a further incentive. So I ended by translating Machado, a short selection of César Vallejo and many poems by Octavio himself. Octavio and I even wrote a bilingual poem together, "Airborn," which we each translated into our own tongue. I simultaneously came to realize just how many of our poets, going back to Chaucer, had been great translators, all the time extending the possibilities of English by introducing new forms and new ideas for poetry. So I went ahead and edited *The Oxford Book of Verse in English Translation*.

INTERVIEWER

And Dryden?

TOMLINSON

Dryden was one of the greatest of our translators. His Virgil and Pope's Homer could do a lot to repair the neglect of classical studies, but then you realize that the kids by and large aren't really equipped for any kind of poetic experience that requires a little historical imagination—seventeenth- and eighteenth-century poetry must sound as foreign to some of them as the originals Dryden and Pope were translating. Not only languages, but historical awareness has suffered in the great dumbing-down.

INTERVIEWER

Are you gloomy about all this?

TOMLINSON

There are the heartening exceptions. And there are the teachers capable of giving students a sense of direction. We had an extraordinary phase at Bristol when Augustan English and French literature of the classical period were being taught together. A brilliant young classicist, a Dryden scholar, suddenly energized the teaching of Augustan poetry, and students were no longer impatiently waiting to abandon all that for the romantics. As part of my own continuing education, I was called in to examine the French—it might be anything from Montaigne to Racine to Baudelaire. Hard work for teachers, of course, but you felt you were fighting back against the know-nothing schools with their lazy abandonment of spelling and grammar and their language teaching that got as far as how to book a hotel room on the other side of the channel. I think the kids performed magnificently—they taught me a lot, both about their chosen authors and about the resilience of the human mind awakened by great literature.

INTERVIEWER

To tackle a related but complementary fact of your life: could you comment on what to an American observer looks like an admirably quaint, almost old-fashioned lifestyle here at the cottage: no telephone and so forth. Do you feel separated from the world?

TOMLINSON

I suppose quaintness is very much in the eye of the beholder. A more affectionate response to this house might be that it's but one example of the endless variety of English vernacular architecture, a lesson in the use of local materials—stone and limewash—and of a tactful relationship with its surroundings. A dangerously old-fashioned lifestyle? I really must fill out for you the sense of what goes on here or from here. For practically forty years I taught in a leading British university in our fifth largest city. We brought up a family of two girls and, like the rest of contemporary humanity, were busy getting them to school, music lessons and friends. We all went to the opera together in Bristol and by the time they began at the Royal Academy of Music, they had seen most of the classics. When we could afford it we went to Italy *en famille* and the world of Renaissance art and architecture awaited us.

INTERVIEWER

And the house itself?

TOMLINSON

Yes, the house. The absence of a telephone didn't prevent us from using the public phone at the top of the hill, or our many friends from coming here—among these, Octavio Paz and his wife, Jaccottet, Attilio Bertolucci (whom I was to translate), German, Spanish, Portuguese and Mexican friends. Brenda and I have traveled all over the world. If you can't find us here, you might have to go to Siena, Lisbon, New York, Toronto or even Kyoto. This house may be our center, but its geographical position has never restricted us or shut us off from the world. We're not in retreat from anything, any more than one is living in Connecticut or Dallas. In fact, this area offers a stimulating range of very sophisticated neighbors, including musicians, writers, art historians who are part of the nation's consciousness. For fifteen years our nearest neighbor was Bruce Chatwin, and those famous books of his underwent much discussion beneath this very roof before they were published. In an hour and twenty minutes we can be in Oxford. In an hour and a half the train gets us to London. It's not North Dakota, you know. But one thing I've left until last. Let me say just this: every day here is a quiet celebration of married love.

INTERVIEWER

Let me return to my earlier inquiry about literary Englishness and Americanness. You are rare in admiring, or paying homage to, both Williams and Stevens. Americans tend to pick sides. Does being British have the advantage of allowing you to admire both of them—and their schools—with no *parti pris*?

TOMLINSON

Perhaps this is a question of generation rather than being British. Marianne Moore admired both, so did Yvor Winters with whatever reservations he had about either. I always thought the redskin-paleface division between them a rather cheap contrast. I suppose all the reams of cogitation Stevens accumulated in his poetry made those of the Objectivist tradition rather impatient, as they did me after a certain point, though there are many fine things in the later poetry too.

INTERVIEWER

What do you get from both of these poets?

TOMLINSON

Both poets—Stevens and Williams—can give you the sense of a sudden dawning freshness, an enlargement of mind and senses like, as Stevens says, "The way, when we climb a mountain, / Vermont throws itself together." He prefers the effect of perspective, whereas for Williams the enlargement is more intimate, as in the unfolding of the flower in "The Crimson Cyclamen," which is closer perhaps to the modern world, to the world of time-lapse photography, as Kenner has suggested. Stevens's vista-effect still carries with it something of the old sublime of the Hudson River school. I like both ways of seeing.

INTERVIEWER

Your remark in the preface to *Collected Poems* that you reached a point where "space represented possibility and where self would have to embrace that possibility somewhat self-forgetfully, putting aside more possessive and violent claims of personality" looks—on the face of it—like standard English *politesse*, an unwillingness to promote the self to the exclusion of other things in the world. It is also a version of a great remark by Elizabeth Bishop: "What one seems to want in art, in experiencing it, is the same thing that is necessary for its creation, a self-forgetful, perfectly useless concentration." Another poet famous for reticence, and eye, description, travel, and so forth: do you feel affinities with her?

TOMLINSON

I've always admired Elizabeth Bishop. In 1956 I asked F.W. Bateson, then editor of *Essays in Criticism*, if I could review the Chatto *Poems*—just out then. His reply was, "We don't want that sort of thing—it's just Marianne Moore and water." So I didn't write on Bishop for several years. I persuaded myself that I disliked the tone of much of her *Questions of Travel* and wrote a rather negative review of it in *Shenandoah*. A pity. I would have liked to meet her. Even in that review I had conceded, "There are few other poets writing who, in the handling of detail, of internal rhyme, of awkward yet convincingly expressive rhythms, show more professionalism." A funny word to use! And the tone, too! Ah, the follies of youth. I think I redeemed them partially, twenty-five years later, with a piece in *Parnassus*. Alas, she was dead by then. Yes, I've felt affinities with her. I could still kick myself for that review in 1966—though I wasn't wholly at fault: I continue to believe that there *was* a self-conscious archness at times that damages the marvelous detail.

INTERVIEWER

At what point did you settle into various congenial poetic forms and habits—the pseudo-elegiac couplets, the various rhyming schemes: your first poems were not like this at all.

TOMLINSON

To carry the longer poems of *Seeing Is Believing*, I invented a mainly four-stress line that would work me free of the track of the iambic pentameter though permit me to modulate towards that if I must. This has lasted me for many years and gave the formal scaffolding for political poems like the one on the death of Trotsky, "Assassin," and, in a book a decade later, "Prometheus," about the Russian revolution. Rhyme was important to such poems, but it was years before I ventured to try rhyming couplets—something that an immersion in Dryden encouraged me to do. In poems like "Assassin" and "Prometheus" rhyme acted as a sound link that must never become too predictable or static. It was a kind of syncopation punctuating the forward progress of an energetic syntax.

INTERVIEWER

This sounds like the language of Donald Davie, yes?

TOMLINSON

I was embodying Donald Davie's description of syntax as "articulate energy"—and underscoring it with rhyme and half-rhyme. There is the clarity and constancy of a four-beat line that also records motion and change, and rhyme plays its unexpected part in the reconciliation (frequently to be canceled) of those opposites. But the underlying factor is that of a fluid but lucid line that continually encounters things and then moves on. What keeps the experience alive is an unclotted diction. The great lesson came from eighteenth-century verse with its verve and clarity—from that and also from the Americans. Not so much Stevens here as Moore and the Pound of "Hugh Selwyn Mauberley." But the line is what matters: it must be supple and it must be lucid. It can be as slim as you like (another lesson from American poetry) or it can marshal many unstressed syllables around its four-stress base. I feel the typical movement of these poems reenacts the way we perceive things—reason and feeling trained on a world that is other than we are.

INTERVIEWER

Can you cite some examples from your work of syntactic thinking, or the way Davie's ideas influenced your own practice, the way you deliberately manipulate syntax when composing; or are you aware, afterwards, of your own unconscious manipulations?

TOMLINSON

Davie's book on syntax coincided with my own conscious rediscovery of it in a poem called "Fiascherino." Look anywhere in my poems and there are longish sentences that go on unwinding and finding out and checking meaning. There you have it—thinking via syntax. Davie awoke me to what I already knew—the power of the sustained sentence in Wordsworth, Coleridge, Cowper, Kleist (the last of these I had experienced at school and can still recite). Without Davie I might not have dug out all I knew. I'm less conscious of manipulation than of playing tunes on the verbal piano, variations on grammatic possibilities. *Playing*, that's the word! There's a lot of play in these games with sound and syntax—often more humorous than readers seem to realize.

INTERVIEWER

What about rhyme? "The Chances of Rhyme" seems like a characteristic *ars poetica*: How much do you leave to chance when composing? When does the rhyme come in?

TOMLINSON

As for those rhyming couplets I mentioned, they are mostly used in poems that have a semihumorous content like "A Doggerel for My Seventieth Birthday." I use a fair amount of half-rhyme in order to undermine the Augustan tone or keep it on its toes.

INTERVIEWER

But rhyme is used for more than just semihumorous purposes.

TOMLINSON

For years my wife and I have noticed a curious thing. If one approaches our house by way of the hillside above it, it is difficult to know exactly what one is looking at. For instance, the road beyond the house at times appears to be a plume of smoke. Recently I took those rhyming couplets—or rather half-rhyming couplets—and tried to convey this experience of ambiguity, which is resolved once you come face to face with the house and enter it. The half-rhyme here, rather than relaxed humor, registers or counterpoints the slip in perception. As for the question of chance that you raise, that too is part of perception. A walk implies a series of chance encounters, although you know pretty well where you're going. These chances are then accepted as part of the day's possibilities. The same thing happens with rhyme. I use rhyme of some description in most of my poems. Before I begin, or simultaneously with starting, I often write out the alphabet on the sheet of paper I'm using, so as to be prompted by a side-glance of the eye. Once one is taken forward on the wave of inspiration, it is surprising how sensitive one becomes to such momentary suggestions, and rhymes fly to one's fingertips from the written-out letters.

INTERVIEWER

Many people—especially those we label landscape poets—think in terms of favorite places. Auden's "In Praise of Limestone" is a locus classicus of this kind of thing. Your landscapes are everywhere: Gloucestershire, Italy, New Mexico, upstate New York. Is this because you participate fully in any landscape where you find yourself, or did you deliberately seek out those you suspected in advance would be hospitable?

TOMLINSON

The Italian poet Giuseppe Conte says that love and travel awake the senses in similar ways. You are alert. You see anew. Places for me have often been happy chances like rhyme. I arrived in the deserts of New Mexico in 1960—still on our first American trip—because the Yeats scholar Donald Pearce, encountered in California, knew someone who lived in Albuquerque and who was deeply knowledgeable about life in the Indian pueblos. We saw many dances and ceremonies in the pueblos. Two years later we went back and have been returning ever since. The moment of our first trip was just in time to catch sight of some of the survivors of the D.H. Lawrence era—Dorothy Brett, Ravagli (Frieda Lawrence's husband), Witter Bynner. On our second trip we went to Mexico itself. In a bookstore there (chance once again!) I found a new volume by Octavio Paz, *Salamandra*, translated some of the poems and we became close friends, meeting with surprising frequency afterwards. I seem to have been following in Lawrence's footsteps. For a time, during my Cambridge years and just after, he was a literary moralist who counted greatly for me. When I found a job in Italy in the early fifties—another complete chance—we were living only a stone's throw from Fiascherino, where Lawrence and Frieda had been in 1913–1914. It had hardly changed. It was a marvelous place of introduction to Italian life. And we still go back there. Upstate New York was another matter of chance—we knew Fenimore Cooper's novels, of course, and we happened to find ourselves in a poetry-reading tour which took us to Colgate, which is no great distance from Cooperstown. All these places—and now I can add Spain and Portugal—I associate with lasting friendships and with renewed visits.

INTERVIEWER

The people, in other words, came first?

TOMLINSON

But you were also asking me about my attitude to landscapes. My landscapes, as you say, are everywhere. However,

I prefer not to be thought of simply as a landscape poet or as a connoisseur of the rural, either. Put it this way: any critic of Cézanne who described him as a painter of country scenes would be moving in the wrong direction. You must begin with the question of style, as in my poems you must begin with the question of tone. They possess what Arnold described as "the tone of the city, of the center." One of their characteristics is their aim of urbanity, in short.

INTERVIEWER

Where have you been happiest?

TOMLINSON

I am as happy in the middle of the deserts of New Mexico and Arizona as I am in the more opulent scenes of Tuscany, but I write of all that in the same idiom in which I write about New York. It would be amusing to make a list of places in my poetry that are simply townscapes: New York itself, Paris, Rome, Budapest, Lisbon, Stoke on Trent (where I was born). And what of the extraordinary landscapes of the marble quarrying region around Carrara? They change every time you see them. The stone villages seem the only stable part of the scene and they, too, piled up on the slopes, take the shape of quarries and are the same color. They are as thrilling to me as Manhattan, and I need all my urbanity of style to define and express the beauty of either place.

INTERVIEWER

So style then becomes a reflection of your vision? And mere scenery is secondary? Keats said "scenery is fine but human nature is finer." I think also of Blake's famous aphorism: "Where man is not, nature is barren."

TOMLINSON

My attitude to landscape, when writing poems, is ultimately a question of style—an urban or urbane style, but the reflection of an ideal *urbs*, of civilization, of what I've learned about the precise fit of word and concept, of the rhythms of the body—particularly while walking—translated into the progress from line to line. But scenery, the pastoral, life in the Cotswolds are not my aim.

INTERVIEWER

A book by the American critic Roger Gilbert, *Walks in the World*, deals with the motif of the poem-as-a-walk, the poet walking and contemplating, and so forth. Your own remarks and habits suggest that you fit into this Wordsworthian vein. Can you remember specific times when poems sprang from things seen or thought of while you were perambulating?

TOMLINSON

I write down lines, phrases, grammatic constructions while perambulating—my sixty-odd notebooks are full of these. Like Nietzsche, I tend to distrust thoughts that have not come to me when in physical motion. The physical motion goes straight into the syntax. I reinvent the sense of physical motion when I start to write and the imagination takes charge.

INTERVIEWER

Is place a matter of spiritual questing for you, or of aesthetic appreciation?

TOMLINSON

I don't know what "aesthetic appreciation" is. I never quested for anything. I'm simply there and I'm bowled over. Surely Conte's comparison with being in love is completely accurate? And, as with love, the question of fidelity arises. One must go back and back and gaze more and more. But aesthetic . . . ?

INTERVIEWER

Your poetry both tacitly and explicitly praises the virtues of moderation—a habit you share with Auden and Horace, our two masters of this tone of voice. Another (I assume) *ars poetica* and personal self-portrait is "Against Extremity," in which you say some harsh things about the so-called confessional poets. I assume you are referring to Sylvia Plath and Anne Sexton although you delicately avoid naming them. How do you separate the created self or the speaker of lyric from the depths of psychoanalytical subjectivity? What sense of self is necessary for poetry, for *your* poetry?

TOMLINSON

I think my kind of poetry is utterly opposed to the sort of solipsism that weaves a fantasy between oneself and the world. Of course, people with various grouses and psychological hang-ups feast on their own view of things. Plath could imagine her own father, whom she had scarcely known, as a Nazi and then transfer this mania to her husband. She is, needless to say, a far more impressive writer than Sexton and with extraordinary verbal intuition. I don't really know "what sense of self is necessary for poetry." Rimbaud is hardly a figure of moderation, but every time I read him, I am overcome once more by the sheer freshness of invention, as if an impregnable innocence had somehow persisted throughout those years of vagabondage.

INTERVIEWER

Rimbaud is hardly one of the first several dozen poets I would assume would come into your list of favorites. Does "freshness of invention" mean that you think of poetry as a heightened version of speech? What do you try to be on your guard against in conceiving and then working through a poem—in terms of diction, I mean.

TOMLINSON

A short time ago you reminded me that my career had gone on for fifty years. I was about to put you right, but then realized that you were indeed right. It is, unbelievably, fifty years since I began. What do I try to be on my guard against? The fact that I exercised that kind of watchfulness at the beginning, so that now I sit down fairly certain that I cured a lot of bad habits more than half a life ago, in the first phase of that fifty-year period. Blake was the problem and his prophetic books. Blake simply lost the bounding wiry line of his lyrics when he came to write those long lines of the prophecies. Without having experienced the discipline of the bounding line, I flung myself into the shapeless fume of putting the world right by repetition. I was also trying to be a painter at that time and attempted to integrate illustrations and text. The illustrations were the better part. The text was nowhere. I had read Whitman too, and my last school prize (the influence of that German teacher) was Nietzsche's *Thus Spake Zarathustra*—fatal from the point of view of diction and its encouragement to be hortatory. Since God was dead, I summoned forth the gods—shades of the weaker side of D.H. Lawrence here. The vatic and the hortatory! What could have been worse? I wanted to pull down the cathedrals and consign them to the graveyard of dead giants. (Of course, I didn't really believe all that, but why did I say it?) Occasionally something of the aphoristic side of Blake came through in the shape of the more symmetrical propositions of *The Marriage of Heaven and Hell*.

INTERVIEWER

A fearful symmetry?

TOMLINSON

But clearly I couldn't achieve a real symmetry until I'd found a line that could be proportioned. To begin with, it had to be shorter. Once I'd got hold of that fact, I quickly learned that you couldn't shout in a short line. I also began to reflect consciously on the use of rhyme. So bit by bit I did the hard work, which freed me for the much harder work of exact expression and a diction that defined what one was talking about as one began to move to the dance of rhyme. After a time it wasn't restraint I was looking for, but melody and clarity. Once the diction of these poems appeared as heightened speech, then I could somehow begin to span the gap between the conceptual qualities of Augustan poetry and the kinetic qualities of a Hopkins, without losing my way in the over-clotted effects that could have been a real danger from that quarter, and evidently were for Dylan Thomas (another influence to avoid, as I soon realized).

INTERVIEWER

This is where some of your American poets must have come in handy.

TOMLINSON

So I finally discovered "Thirteen Ways of Looking at a Blackbird" and that became my talisman and my way out of the romantic jungle. I discovered Marianne Moore's "The Jerboa" that "makes fern-seed / foot-prints with kangaroo speed" and started to see what rhyming might be. But why does it take so long? I had the Moore in a secondhand copy of Michael Roberts' *Faber Book of Modern Verse*, acquired as a student. Why couldn't one see at a glance that this was more congenial than all that Blakean pother? It took years.

INTERVIEWER

To the extent that you are self-conscious about your compositional methods, how can you tell when you have got hold of something, or when something has got hold of you? How do you know when a poem is finished? Is it merely, in Valéry's memorable phrase, abandoned?

TOMLINSON

I'm not sure that Valéry merely abandoned "Le Cimetière Marin." The French are over-full of memorable rhetoric. I've always found a certain discrepancy between some of Valéry's prose statements and the verse. If ever a poem had *finish*, surely "Ébauche d'un serpent" did. So does "Palme" in a different way. But you're asking me about my own methods of composition. The methods differ so much I hardly know where to begin to answer. Sometimes I know exactly how I want to end. Sometimes I get stuck on the very last line. Occasionally I've started over again by changing the meter. Sometimes I've found a poem hiding itself in the middle of something that ended up in the wastepaper basket. I know when I've finished all right, but I don't always know *how* to finish. Then sometimes I finish and decide the final line or lines are superfluous. The process somewhat reminds me of making a film and all the labor of the cutting room.

INTERVIEWER

Are you an avid moviegoer?

TOMLINSON

Apart from literary efforts, I spent much time on seeing films and writing film scripts early in my career. Richard Swigg, in his remarkable book *Charles Tomlinson and the Objective Tradition* has shown in some detail the way both images from and the actual sound track of *Citizen Kane* have percolated into the poem "Assassin," for example. I even tried to get a job in films. The concentration on all that visual material surely brought something to bear on the shape of the poems themselves—a certain concision, the effect of the single shot.

INTERVIEWER

Because of your bookishness, your vision, your travels, you seem enormously curious about the world. (This is not always true—even of great poets.) Do you see the world as discrete objects, part of a vast plan, symbols in some Baudelairean series of correspondences, evidence of meaning or design? Or do you see it—whether spiritually or aesthetically—as a cause for celebration?

TOMLINSON

I see the world in all its variety as a cause for celebration, for exaltation. I detest the idea of symbols in a series of correspondences. Let things be what they are, and that is enough for me. The trouble with some of Hopkins's poems is that he arbitrarily gives symbolic meanings to his subject matter. How differently he works in the notebooks, where the forms of nature are often left in all their this-ness and he doesn't force them into symbolic cohesion. His poem "Epithalamion" (a title he obviously tacked on once he'd decided on the symbolic meaning), begins with a lovely evocation of a river in which boys are bathing. By the close he decides what the scene means: "Wedlock. What the water? Spousal love." Then he gets stuck and can't finish the piece, incapable of settling for what is there and abandoning his symbolic interest.

INTERVIEWER

Your lovely poem "For a Godchild" suggests a strongly anti-Catholic or anti-clerical streak, and a strong commitment to what at least in the States goes under the name *secular humanism*. You say you must make sure that the child

. . . ponders well
what she takes to be
the dues of deity—
and learn that a god
who harbours anger where
thirst has no slaking,
eyes no ease,
is either of her own
or others' making.

I wonder whether this attitude is as unfashionable as it is in America. We are the most churchgoing, God-fearing, religious people in the Western world, by the way.

TOMLINSON

My poem is a Blakean response to other people's attempts to rigidify the unknowable. You remember the way Blake speaks of "the mind-forg'd manacles" and how, in a poem like "The Human Abstract," the tree that bears the fruits of deceit isn't to be found in nature, but in the human brain. I tell my godchild that she should distrust a god who, like Dante's, encourages you to think you shouldn't "wipe / a sinner's eyes in hell." The existence of that god "is either of her own / or others' making," like the mind-forg'd manacles and the fruits of deceit.

INTERVIEWER

How would you characterize your own *weltanschauung*?

TOMLINSON

I'm not so sure that your "secular humanism" or "a strongly anti-Catholic streak" quite cover what you so flatteringly call my *weltanschauung*. My first full-scale book, *Seeing Is Believing*, contains a rather Kantian poem, "In Defence of Metaphysics." I live—my poems live—in a world of presences that touches on the unknowable, where "to name the Name" seems crudely premature. I think, too, that a secular humanist would scarcely begin a poem as I do with

It was the song of Adam
the devil envied most,
and the song of Adam
that Adam lost . . .

and go on to talk of "the steady spate / and the hidden source," or in another book, *Annunciations*, which has Lorenzo Lotto's great annunciation on its cover, mention "the sheen / drop by drop / still spilling-over / out of the grail of origin." A Catholic friend who had been reading a review of one of my books remarked, "I see the reviewer takes you to task for your atheism." The reviewer was Michael Edwards, one of our most learned Christian critics, and what he actually said was, "The ethic of these poems is not Christian, but neither is it secular." In writing poems, I do not think that if I say this, I am disqualified from saying that. I'm not a Catholic, but there is much in the Catholic tradition that is precious to me—many Italian churches, and indeed most of Dante himself.

INTERVIEWER

Let's end with something more specific, which also returns us to the start of our discussion. The poet of *Seeing Is Believing* was also a painter, perhaps a long time ago. I know you have discussed your own work as a visual artist in various prose works, but I wonder whether you might say how your earlier efforts worked in tandem with your literary ones. Did you ever think of yourself as a serious artist, or as just a Sunday dabbler?

TOMLINSON

Can you *imagine* me ever being less than a serious artist? As for a Sunday dabbler! The suggestion leaves me breathless and sputtering.

INTERVIEWER

I mean no offense. Please go on.

TOMLINSON

The second phase of my artistic efforts (1968–1978) coincides with and expresses what I call "a season in Eden" (the opposite of Rimbaud's *Saison en Enfer*—he, for me, has often been a touchstone for what cannot any longer be undertaken, but also for sheer vivacity). I moved from very exact pencil drawings to equally exact collages that utilized chance effects—decalcomania.

INTERVIEWER

The chances of rhyme went, so to speak, hand-in-hand with the chances of hand and eye? How did the work progress?

TOMLINSON

It resulted in a 1978 Arts Council exhibition at the Hayward Gallery, which toured in England, Wales and Canada. A book appeared, *In Black and White*, badly produced because the publisher had never done an art book before, but with a splendid introduction by Octavio Paz, who had always encouraged my visual activities. A second book, *Eden*, excellently produced, appeared from a small press in Bristol; a third, *Words and Images*, attempted to show how the rocks and light of my poetry had discovered a new dimension. In 1978 I realized that my season in Eden was at an end.

INTERVIEWER

Why? How come?

TOMLINSON

I do not know. Probably because I was doing too much, with poetry, graphics, and full-time teaching and research. You cannot anyhow stay in Eden for long, and ten years isn't bad. My poetry benefited from my residence there in becoming, I think, more open to chance encounters with artistic possibilities. I cannot repeat this phase now because I am virtually blind in my left eye—I no longer possess the sense of visual inevitability that was once my dearest gift. I've spoken of a "second phase."

INTERVIEWER

This sounds mysterious, positively Yeatsian.

TOMLINSON

I didn't mean to be mysterious, but this seemed far more important than the first one, when I was copying Blake's prophetic books. The interesting fact is that the illustrations to these, or whatever one wants to call them, were far purer than the rhetoric of the text itself, and this purity led me by stages into a breathable atmosphere.

INTERVIEWER

Purity is another Donald Davie word.

TOMLINSON

Yes. This purity led me also to produce individual pictures. I worked much in color then and exhibited in London at the Leicester Galleries, Gimpel Fils and the Brook Street Gallery. Curiously enough a recent look at these early images (the first in years) made me reflect on how they had somehow played a hidden role in the emergence and invention of my later Eden. This first phase began in the late forties and early fifties, continuing up to about 1958.

INTERVIEWER

That was then; this is now. Can you summarize the most recent phase, and say something not only about where you have been but also where you are now?

TOMLINSON

Well, let me try to put things into some sort of perspective. I'm still immensely grateful to those poets who encouraged me when I was young. Williams, Marianne Moore, Louis Zukofsky, George Oppen. I took down Moore from the shelf again only this week—what audacity, what accuracy of phrase! The encouragement I owe to those Americans helped me to speak as an Englishman, helped me to find my own voice. The sense of that support stayed with me right across the years, and I think it is that sense of people who have stood by me—my wife above all—that enabled me to get through this last, ghastly, half-blind year. I kept to my writing and the sheer current of it carried me forward. Then came a pause: I'd temporarily exhausted my supplies. Then something unexpected happened, only two or three weeks ago. We took a friend to Somerset to look at the country where we'd once lived at the start of my literary career. An enormous elation, partly caused by the sheer beauty of the place and the grandeur of the great cathedral at Wells, swept over me. So much for secular humanism! I was writing a poem a day—including a couple of long ones. Everything I encountered seemed to turn into poetry. Last week—only last week—I realized I must rein myself in, because next week we are off to Tokyo, where I shall be giving a reading. So in this state of enforced restraint, with the energies burning in my very fingertips, I can say, as I enter my seventy-second year, that I have never felt so full of possibility. The promise of the future has never seemed so fecund. I need no longer go on about the failure of that operation. I think I've come through.

—Willard Spiegelman

Portfolio

Americana

Kcho

La Isla de mis suenos II (The Island of My Dreams), 1996.
Charcoal on paper, 59¼″ × 60¼″.

Columna Infinita, 1996. Charcoal on paper, 85″ × 59¼″.

T.C., 1997. Charcoal on paper, 92″ × 59″.

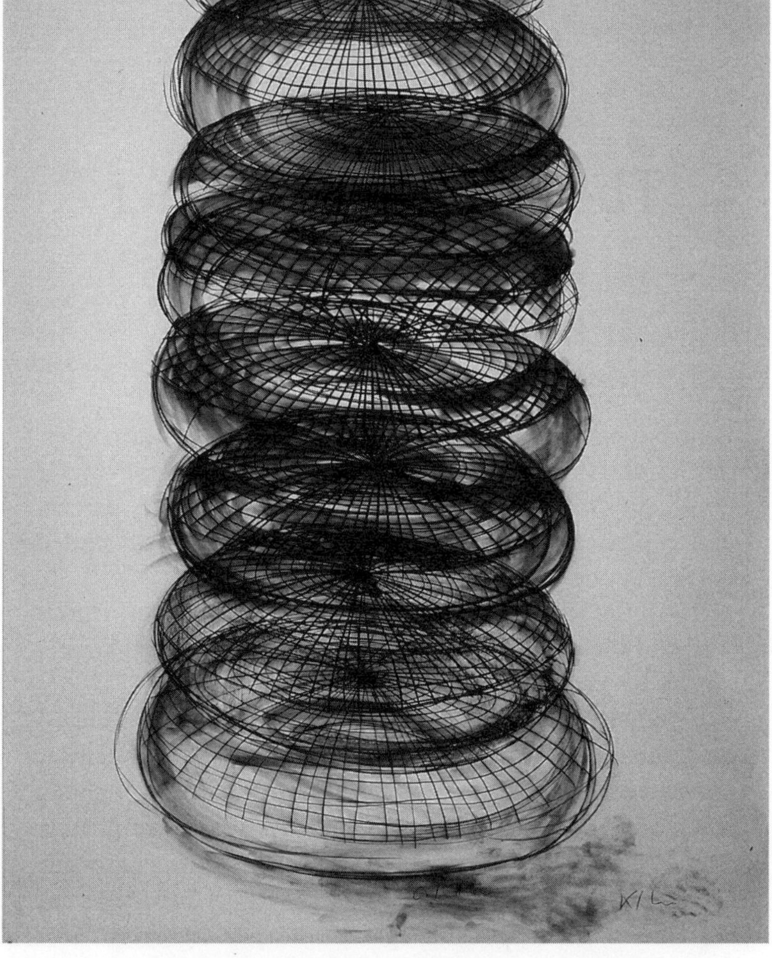

Columna Infinita, 1996. Charcoal on paper, 87″ × 59¼″.

The Second Gardener

Michael Jacot

He put his foot on the rusted railway line among the nettles, thistles and cacti. In this way he managed to see over the rotted ends of the planks that had been part of the derelict station platform, and into the dark earth of the small garden shaded by the sycamore.

It was the wet season. The morning was luminous, the air crisp and the temperature pleasant. He took in a deep breath, closing his eyes, and then let out a heavy sigh.

A persistent melancholy rumbled inside him. In the eleven weeks he and Gossart had been put in charge of the railway station a despair had festered. The garden had been his solitary relief. More perhaps than a relief. More too than a perfunctory religious rite, such as Gossart practiced three times a day while he lived. It was a food, something as vital to his life as the old rifle now propped up against the peeling green door behind the garden, near Gossart's shallow grave.

He gave another sigh and opened his eyes once more,

examining the graceless rows of wandering furrows he had made while planting. They wormed their way like wrinkles on an old man's brow, dodging rocks and other impediments, their seeds fermenting, awaiting warmth.

Up on the mountain ridge to the east, which shone in the palest shade of translucent blue, a color almost too powerful to hold in your eye at that short distance, spring had already arrived, and among the jagged peaks, dark patches of green had come to life. The mountains were probably a month ahead of the spot where his garden lay. But soon the stream that flowed behind the railway station and once gave water to the war-destroyed village nearby would dry up under the first week of spring sun, and the sycamore would become the garden's savior. The way he had planted, banking to hold the water, would also help. Only one year ago he had watched his father, the head gardener at the big house, making the same sort of furrows for the same reason.

The sky was out today and somewhere high in it he heard a jet aircraft. He saw it now, its feathered white tail eventually being eaten by the sky. It was heading for the gulf or somewhere where the war was, or where it wasn't. How could he tell? And what was he supposed to do if he could tell? Take up that old rifle and try to shoot it down? He sighed again. The whole war, with its planes, tanks and big guns was only as far as his eye could see. It was there or not when he heard shooting. Gossart used to say that the war was only as long as his arm. No farther. And that was logical.

He strode across the creaking planks of the old platform and took his helmet from its place of decoration on the tip of the rifle. Then he walked through the building and down to the muddy slope of the stream. He dipped the helmet in the water and filled it. He had once tried to dig a trench from the stream to the garden, but the railway station was built on rock. So each morning and evening he fed the garden from his helmet, sprinkling the light soil like someone sowing seed.

Careful not to step on Gossart's still soft grave, he threw

the last of it against the station foundations, knowing that the stones would hold the moisture and the earth would eventually suckle from it.

The space for the garden was limited by the tree roots and rocks, and he'd like to have made it larger for there was a lot more seed inside the freight room. It lay with many other commodities that had been sent for the villagers, which no one ever claimed. The people were all dead, except those who had managed to flee. He had broken open the room with his knife and found bags of flour, cans of brown stew probably made from mutton, cartons of unlabeled food, which turned out to be dried eggs, and tins of cigarettes, as well as seeds.

He walked back along the platform to where he could still dangle his booted feet over the edge and kick at the nettles. It was the action of a despondent man, and until something happened to change his mood there was little he could do about it, except nurse the feeling in the bottom of his belly and make sure it did not rise in fits of rage. The feeling did not come from his present surroundings. It came from his relationship with his father, which had come to a climax over a year ago. It would bubble angrily until nature had purged him.

He surveyed the horizon, hoping that something had changed in the night. To the north of the station there were points and a big lever to switch them. One line went on through the abandoned village where few houses still had roofs on them and ended in a town some eighty-seven kilometers away. The other line went towards the mountain ridge and skirted the end of it making its way to the sea.

He and Gossart had been given standing orders to guard the place because of the line to the sea. It was thought also that the enemy might want to retake the railway station as a vantage point. Both sides grabbed greedily to prove possession. There was no logic to it. It was always some commandant's strategy. It was the war. And even if it had logic, surely the enemy would not use the railway, which was in a state of ruin? They would use the sand road on the other side of the scrub, half a kilometer away. It could carry trucks and other heavy vehicles. There was no mention of it in the standing orders given to Gossart. Perhaps the important leaders had forgotten there was a perfectly good road to the sea. The stupidity of it all made his stomach churn again and he looked back over his shoulder, towards the garden. It was now under the heat of the day. The sun shadowed the recent imprints of his own boots, made as he watered with the helmet. The shadows gave the scene a permanency like fossils in brown rock.

Each day about this time he went inside the ticket office and opened one of the cans of food that he had stacked under the window ready to use. In the evenings a breeze rustled past the old sycamore and filtered through the broken glass, cooling the humid cans.

Sometimes he fished out Gossart's big billycan from his pack, which rested beside the bedroll on which Gossart had spent his last eight days crying out with a pain that made his words animal sounds and caused his fingers to tear out lumps of his own flesh. It was horrible seeing Gossart die, hearing him and being able to do so little for him. It went on day and night as his skin tightened over the bones and turned yellow and then became dark leather. At times in the moonlight he could see Gossart's blue eyes, bright jewels, searching the ceiling for help.

He took Gossart's billycan today. He went out towards the stream and used his knife to jab open the can. Then he took out his cigarette lighter and put it up against a pile of dry scrub grass, throwing sticks on it as it flared, heating the contents of the can and then swallowing the brown sticky mixture as quickly as he could so that it would fill his stomach without the need to taste it. Afterwards he swilled out his mouth at the stream. Lastly he walked around the south end of the building through his garden. Nothing had changed of course in his one hour of absence, but he might have missed a small chalky pebble, an ant track or the spiky footprints of the *tik-tikki*, a small green leaf-eating lizard.

He had made a trowel, a big thing, dark, dull and metallic, by hammering flat one of the food cans with a rock. It was well over thirty centimeters, including the handle made of a narrow piece of lead water pipe, and a powerful weapon against beetles and other crawling invaders. He unhooked it from the holster that was meant to carry his revolver. The revolver was now somewhere in the scrub towards the stream. One night when Gossart's howls had been too frustrating, he had put his revolver to Gossart's temple, thinking to put him out of his misery, like any dog or horse. But Gossart's bright eyes had caught his and the anger that swirled around in his stomach had reached his mouth in cowardly bile. He had thrown the revolver through the broken window and watched it bounce into the scrub. That night he went back to sleep, his head covered in his khaki winter pullover to deaden Gossart's constant stream of half-words and moans, and cursing his weakness at not being able to finish the job.

Under the sycamore he dug around with the makeshift trowel, more at play than at serious work. When he looked up from it, there was a man on a motorcycle coming across the scrub from the sand road. The man was about half a kilometer away, but the sound of the motorcycle was loud. He reached out, groping for his rifle, but it was nowhere near enough for him to grab. He sat on his haunches, protected by the sycamore and waited. The man and his machine were clouded in sand now. Even the noise of the engine seemed muted.

The cloud of sand rolled away into the dry scrub as the man came to a stop thirty meters away where the railway line ran along a small embankment. He saw the man survey the ruined railway station, thinking perhaps that it was deserted. He propped up the motorcycle and walked up the embankment to survey more closely the creaking old wooden structure. Now he revealed his army insignia.

From under the sycamore he stood up and waved his trowel, stepping forward into the light and shouting. "You are one of us. Ha!"

The man beside the motorcycle waved back and shouted something incomprehensible. He came and placed his foot on the far bank, ten meters away. "Hey soldier. So you are still here?" The motorcyclist was a corporal. His saddlebags bulged with messages and war secrets. He said, "We are retreating, they sent me to tell you both."

"To where? To where are we retreating?"

"I don't know, my friend. And if I did I would not tell you. You are to abandon this place. Tell your comrade. It is an order. I was sent."

"Name the man, comrade."

"A commandant. Very important. Too important for you to know his name. Just get out of here fast."

"But which way? To the mountains?"

"Yes. To the mountains. Follow the stream."

"Then the enemy is near?"

"On the road I could smell them. Hurry. I am sent to save your skin. Tell your comrade. To the mountains."

He felt the need to keep the man in conversation. He had spoken to no one but himself and to the garden since Gossart's death. "You must be thirsty. Let me fill your canteen. The stream is clean."

"My canteen is full. I am in a hurry."

"Rest a moment. Smoke a cigarette with me, comrade? I have cigarettes. Tins of them. Not Albanian cigarettes. They were made in Turkey or Egypt. I can't read the writing."

"There is no time. I have most important business. Take your cigarettes to the mountains. Tonight they will be here."

He tried to think of some other ruse to keep the man who was now taking something out of one of his saddlebags. "How is my friend General Ruskovitch?" he asked.

"How should I know? All I know of the war is there is not enough gasoline for the bike. Here," the man went on, stooping to place a box on the railway line, "that's for you."

"Food?" He laughed, for it could never be food. It was an oily, greasy sort of box. It was an army weapon of some sort. "Did you hear the joke about General Ruskovitch, comrade?

He was standing under the shower and his orderly was soaping him . . ."

"I have no time for jokes. This package contains a land mine, some grenades and copper wiring."

"What am I supposed to do with grenades? Kill *tik-tikkis*?"

"You are to blow up this godforsaken place before you leave. Sergeant Gossart will know how to fix it. That is an order."

"Why blow it up? Who would use it?"

"The enemy. Look, I don't know. Don't give me any shit. It must be for some reason. How should I know? Or you for that matter. It is an order. All you have to think about is carrying it out. So make sure you blow it to hell. And place this land mine under the railway track so that if a train comes this way, it too will go sky high."

"Nobody in his right mind would . . . "

The motorcyclist wagged his finger at him as if he was brandishing a gun, "There *is* no reason. So shut up. If there was a reason for everything in my message bags, I'd go mad trying to wonder why there were reasons of that sort in this shitty war."

"You are serious?" he said, coming across the line and picking up the heavy box.

The man was already back on the saddle of his machine.

"Stop thinking. Just be a soldier. Save your own soul or you'll become a raving lunatic. To *someone*, blowing up this rat hole is important. It is a military target. *Someone* had a good idea. In the war all ideas are good. It's only after the war that some seem stupid."

"That's a ridiculous way to think, corporal. Are you sure about the water? I could offer you some mutton stew?"

The corporal was now turning his bike to face the distant road, its engine revving like water pipes in an old hothouse. The man waved and almost immediately was covered with sand again, "Don't forget to explain to Sergeant Gossart," the man shouted.

"When I see him I will," he said. "He's resting."

He stood for what seemed to be many minutes watching him disappear and as the man reached the road and turned north he sighed again. He went inside with the bombs. He sat, and retold the whole conversation, describing it to himself, from the moment that the motorcyclist had arrived in the sand cloud to the moment he left again also covered in sand. He stopped to analyze each sentence. What had he meant by this? And what did that mean? But he was putting off thinking about the most worrisome part of it all. The order to blow this place to hell. Of all the damn stupid orders of this war that was the most meaningless. At first he thought he would ignore the whole business. Blot out the fact that the corporal and the war had ever come near him, just as he might try to blot out a nightmare. But after some thought he knew he could be shot if he disobeyed. So he spent most of the afternoon trying to work it out and yet always coming up without a decision, without even a finish to his train of thought.

The sun went down early at the railway station because the mountain interrupted its rays. But before it disappeared he saw on the sand road a convoy. Trucks, tanks, guns, rocket launchers. And in trucks heading the convoy were several blue berets. And a large Red Cross truck. Then a van with an American flag on it. He scratched his head and wondered. They did not stop. They were the enemy. The insignias were not those of comrades in arms. Something big was happening. The war was back.

When he had packed his kit bag with food, he stuffed his pockets with his few personal belongings, the letter from his father apologizing for his behavior, a rosary of his mother's, a certificate from the owner of the big house to say he was permitted in certain areas of the grounds because he was the official second gardener, a scratchy army-issue pencil and the small notepad onto which soldiers were supposed to write reports of suspicious activity.

The sight of the large convoy with its American flags and rocket launchers had shaken him out of the placid routine he had fallen into since Gossart's death. Reluctantly he knew he must move. He spent some time in the garden with the kit bag on his shoulder and his pack slung loosely on his back. In that period he almost persuaded himself that it might be just as safe to hide by the stream nearby. He hated the thought of leaving the garden. But, he eventually told himself, nothing much would happen to it for a month or so. He prayed that no one would take over the station or touch the garden. There was little likelihood of it. Who would want to take possession of such a run-down, dirty place. Even the enemy would find it too filthy. And the railway itself was unusable. Besides the mine was one of those Russian models. They called them A-43s. If any vehicle or a platoon of soldiers touched it, the whole place would go up and they'd never even find the legs and arms or heads of the bodies.

He had the grenades in his pack. He looked at each one carefully, examining it as if buying fruit in the market. He would never use them to demolish the building. He made that decision almost immediately while tossing one from hand to hand. Two of them were what his explosives instructor called *double-tuners*. They had twice the force of the others. One of these he put back in his pack, the other he laid on the platform, gently resting it against the wall so that it would not roll. The two small "pineapples" he replaced in their pouch, which he slung through the plastic handle from his belt. The big monster resting against the wall he took gingerly into his hands.

He sat on the platform, his back against the wall and started to doctor it. If he was able to remove the explosive he could fling it onto the station roof and create an alibi. To disobey an order was punishable by instant death. But if he could show that he had tossed the grenade onto the roof and it had never exploded, then he hadn't disobeyed. They had given him faulty equipment. But you had to be careful in the doctoring. Gossart had shown him. Gossart had spent time blowing up bridges with the engineers. You had to have the skill and patience of a watchmaker. He went through the sequence of mechanical operations quickly to remind himself. First you took the bomb in your left palm, the handle snugly locked between your thumb and second finger. Then you withdrew the split pin that held the handle in place. From then on you had to keep a firm grip on the handle for if it fell off or slipped, you had five seconds to get rid of the grenade before it blew you to small pieces. The explosion always spurted up like a water spout and the best protection was to fall flat on your face nearby and allow the main blast to blow out above you. With the tip of his knife he eased the split pin out and took it in his teeth.

The explosive powder was in a chamber at the bottom of the grenade. It was held there by an inch-thick screw cap with a locking device. When he buried Gossart he had taken the ring of keys off his belt. He could easily see the key he needed now. It was a cork-shaped piece of metal with inverted lugs that clamped into the lugs on the grenade's screw cap. He tried putting normal pressure on the screw cap but it wouldn't budge. His fingers were already beginning to strain at the pressure of his grip. Painfully he tightened his hold on the handle. He tried again to remove the cap. He held his breath as he did when he lifted a heavy load of earth. And still it would not budge. He examined it closely. It was rusted in. He gave one more powerful twist. The key slipped over the lugs and the grenade jumped in his hand. He slammed it back in place. He was breathing in uneven gulps, sweat running into his eyes.

He put his left wrist against the wall to steady it. His fingers whitened and the strain on the muscles traveled down to his forearm. And yet he still could not move it. He took the pin from his teeth and tried to replace it. One prong of the pin had sprung so wide that it would never go back in its safety slip. He sat against the wall and held the damn thing between his two hands, looking out over the sand and thinking. He could throw it into the stream and run like hell. For a split second he relaxed the grip of his right hand and placed it as support for the left, which was bloodless. He tried to relax the left. But the hand was clamped like a vice around his fingers. It would never leave his hand in time if he threw it into the stream. He picked up his knife again and used the bone handle to tap gently against the screw cap, turning his face away in case it triggered the thing. But nothing happened. His temper rose. The latent anger overcame logic. He hit the cap hard.

What to do? He stood up. If he ran down the platform he might get his blood circulating in the left hand and be able to throw the thing onto the railway line. As he started to run he saw himself in the broken windows looking like a crazy man with a flaming cooking pan in his hands. In that split second he wished he hadn't looked, for he fell. A nail or a broken board got him. For a count of five he thought, Death. Then he began to laugh. The handle was still in his hand and the grenade was rolling into the ticket office. He flung himself against the door post and waited for the explosion. It never came. Minutes passed, it seemed. Then he looked. The grenade was against the counter. He laughed again. Either his fooling around with the cap had defused it or it was a dud.

Rubbing his still painful hand he ran back to the garden where he had his kit bag. He was still thinking there would be a bang. But he had botched it somehow. He took the two small grenades and threw them onto the roof, without taking out the pins. "I threw the grenades commandant but they were duds." It was a joke now that the tension was leaking out of him. It was the best joke of the whole goddamn war.

He had the one grenade left in his pack, and a small deadly looking Mauser that had been Gossart's pride in his pocket. He left his heavy old rifle. He spent a few minutes parting the scrub with his boot to see if his own revolver was near there, but he could not find it. He picked up his makeshift trowel and dug it hard into the end of a furrow. He would be back. He would need it. Let no one enter that garden until he came back. In three, maybe four weeks, they would advance again. That was the way the war was fought. Forward and backward. Forward and backward. He'd know if anyone came through the garden while he was on the mountains; he would know in the same way that someone knows a burglar has been in the house when he returns home.

When he had walked up the stream for three hours or more, he stopped. There was a bombed bridge. It would be shelter for the night. He was tired, but not hungry. He had never looked back. But he knew the station stood as he had left it. A pale moon hung over his head. You could read by it. There was a notice on the side of the bridge in steel letters. It said in old-fashioned script, "Anyone who defaces this bridge will be hanged or otherwise executed according to the law."

The air was chilled and damp, but when it later started to rain, he was glad of the arch of the bridge and he rejoiced thinking that there might be rain on the garden. Then he slept. By midday next he was in the mountains—he had climbed several hundred feet, maybe over a thousand, still following the stream as the corporal had ordered.

Soon he was high enough to be hidden in the pines and spruce, which grew in abundance at this height. The shards of rock up above were now green needles with rich earth valleys in between. The air was filled with the scent of cedar and moss. He thought he could smell strawberries and loganberries. He ran his boot through the scrub on the bank of the stream searching for them. It was already spring up here, as he anticipated. Miniature white plants of a kind he had never seen before sprouted from crevices. He found a spot bedded in dry flinty chips beside the fast water. He pushed into it with his knife and saw that it was dry down to as far as he cared to go. He stamped on the surface to make a firm foundation and cut spruce boughs to place under his bedroll so that it rested on them like a cozy, cushioned island. Above it, leaning against the solid rock face, he built a shelter of pine branches. It was a burrow he could crawl into like a badger. And it gave him a sudden leap of pleasure to see it. He shouted, "Ahoy! You are a fine creation." And his shout startled an animal farther up the bank—a mountain hare.

All you needed to catch a mountain hare was a short length of green wood, some sweet grass and a loop of wire. Of course you could shoot it, too. But he had only two clips of ammunition for Gossart's Mauser, and the copper wire the corporal had left him to fuse the mine was long enough to stretch once again across the railway tracks, so he had cut it. He had about two meters of it in his pack.

For the first time in months he began to feel good. That night he built a small fire and heated some of the brown stuff from the cans he had packed. It tasted much better, harder and not as slimy. Afterwards he sat and watched the fire struggle to keep alive, listening to the excitement of the water as it rushed down towards the garden he missed so much.

He saw himself fifteen years ago, when he carried water from the stream beside the big house to fill the drinking tanks, a bucket at the end of each arm of the wooden yoke stretched across his shoulders. For almost five years he had remained the water boy, living in the barn with his father, who by then was first gardener.

The owner of the big house by the sea liked him, seeing the courage he put into his work and the honesty in his face. When the position of third gardener became vacant, he gave it to him. As he told his father, the taciturn man smiled and said gruffly, "You are growing up. But remember the honor of the family. That is more important than your new position. More important than money even."

A year later the second gardener died in a horrible accident. He got caught in the feeders of a tar boiler when they were putting in fence posts. He died in boiling tar. And once again the owner promoted him from third gardener to second gardener. His father did not smile. "You are too young. Have you remembered what I told you about the family honor?"

From then on he began to dislike his father for his lack of love and understanding, and he poured all his own love into the work, suffering his father's silent moods and glances of distrust.

The fire was dead now, he nodded to himself: it was all a

long time ago. And yet it was still all there beside him. At that point he crawled into his nest and slept without waking until the dawn, for he did not want to think about his father anymore that night. It always became an angry story if he continued.

For several weeks he lived in the pine shelter and the long mountain spring settled in around him bringing berries and dandelion leaves to go with the hares he caught. When the mosquitoes began to buzz in his ears, he realized that in the valley there must be spring though he could see nothing of it. The railway line was out of sight behind the pines. And there came a day when the sun was so hot he had to take off his clothes and wash them in the stream. When he put them back on a couple of hours later he was overwhelmed by a wish to go back. Surely there could be no harm in that? Nor any danger? He had heard no war. No man had jumped out from the trees and threatened to kill him. He ought to risk going back for a day to take a long look, secretly, from the other side of the stream, a mere look.

Three days later he found he had been thinking of little else other than going back. The next day, after spending a sleepless night thinking about it, he packed up his belongings. Remaining were seven cans of the brown stew and a tin of mutton. He dug into the bank of the stream and buried them. Then he sat down to smoke. The burial of the food recalled his digging of Gossart's grave.

This led him to remember how Gossart became ill. He felt uneasy, worried about that again. One more look at the grave would assure him that he had cleansed some of his guilt for Gossart's death by building a decent burial place, safe from jackals and desert foxes. Gossart had not been a good man to live with. But that was not all his fault. He was an orphan and it had made him too strict in observing the law. His life was a religion. Not only at prayer three times a day on the small mat he unrolled with such precision, but in every movement and thought. The washing of his hands before eating, the cleansing of his billycan, the meticulous arrangement of his clothing beside his bedroll. At first it was foreign to a man who had been brought up in the end of a barn. Later it was an irritation. A suppressed irritation. For Gossart was a sergeant and his immediate boss.

In the first week of their occupation of the railway station he had come upon the storeroom where the parcels of freight were hidden. The cigarettes, the canned food and the seeds. With an armful of samples he excitedly placed them in front of Gossart who was seated at the rickety old table in the waiting room, its top scarred by the heavy stamping machine used to validate tickets and now discolored by purple marks of indelible ink.

"Where'd you get these?" Gossart asked.

"It's a lucky find, isn't it? There's a lot more in the freight room."

"How did you find them?" Gossart was polishing his belt. He didn't look up.

"I broke the lock with my knife," he said, showing it still in his hand. He threw a packet of seeds in front of Gossart.

"Then you stole them?"

"Who is there to receive them? The village is deserted. I'm going to make a garden. There are fifty packets of seeds."

"But they are not yours."

"Then who do they belong to?"

Gossart looked up, "To someone. Not you. Perhaps to God."

Gossart's remark about God heated his simmering rage. He stabbed his knife towards the packet of seeds meaning to secure it and drag it to him. The knife went into Gossart's arm as his hand was already over the seed packet. The wound was not deep but blood spread from it.

"I'm sorry. I did not mean to touch you, Gossart."

Gossart was holding his wrist, his eyes on the blood. "The first-aid kit. It's under my pillow. *Ty hlupak.*"

He bound up the arm and again apologized, the rage having subsided, and guilt, just as painful, having taken its place. Gossart did not speak. He stared and rolled back on to his bedroll, his eyes fixed on the seed packet, which he clutched close to his chest. Gossart did not eat that evening, but he prayed. During the night he could hear Gossart moaning. The next morning it was obvious he was delirious, drinking dry three billycans filled with water from the stream. By the following Monday, when he tried to change the dressing, Gossart snarled and pushed him away. The arm was swollen and red as an apple.

Four days later his blood system became poisoned. His skin was a yellow parchment, then patches of leather brown appeared and spread until he was just a pitiful sight of bones and skin stretched like roasted chicken.

Up on the mountain he knew he had to look once more at Gossart's grave. It was important, he told himself. He had to make sure he had done right by the man, a salve for his guilt because of his murderous bout of anger.

Going back he followed the river. He walked nervously. He was in enemy territory. And he had no wish to get back into the war. Even when he came to the deserted village there was not a soul around, although there were places where fires had been made for cooking, some tracks of vehicles and some clumsy footprints. When he could see the railway station he stopped, hidden in the scrub. He waited for dawn.

As a red rim lit the eastern edge of the railway station, he got a shock and he once more became boiling with rage. Someone was inside the building. He saw a light. Perhaps a candle and the shadow of a man against the wall of the ticket office.

The pale dawn and the shadow of a man brought back the picture of his father. It had been a similar dawn. A similar invasion of his life. He had come into the barn where his father sat, a tumbler of slivovitz before him and his rifle across the table. He was to go hunting.

For his father to see, he waved with pleasure a fistful of *koruna.*

"Where did you get that money?" his father asked, eyes burning.

"I was watering the azaleas under the living room window of the big house. The lady gave the money to me."

"What lady? His new wife?"

"Yes, her. You are angry."

"Why did she give it you?" His father stood up slowly, one hand rubbing the stock of his rifle.

"She said I was not to say."

"Why, son?" The father leaned forward.

"She was with this man, not her husband, and I was to take this money and buy something for myself, but to say nothing."

"She gave you the money to bribe you?"

"No. She was being kind."

"And you took it with a smile?"

"Of course. We can buy clothes."

"What did I tell you about family honor?" His father stepped silently around the table, crouched like an animal stalking. His father still believed in the centuries of family laws he was bred with. "To take a bribe is a great dishonor," he said quietly.

To his father family loyalty was as essential as tribal loyalty, and for tribal loyalty they were now fighting a bloody war. His father raised the rifle at his son and as he started to run from the barn he heard the shot hit the doorpost. It was a deer rifle and was more deadly than the weapon the army gave him.

He kept running, running until the sun was well into the heavens. He reached the town and immediately joined the army. Killing was just. Killing was necessary. His father believed it. The army told him it was so. He could not bring himself to believe it.

The intruder inside the station began to pace down the rotted platform towards the garden. He could see him only in flashes through the broken window, the enemy army's insignia glinting occasionally.

He held his breath and lay like a dog, watching. Noiselessly he took out Gossart's Mauser. The invader had his back to him. He was peeing in his garden. Once again rage came to him. He had to steady the Mauser with both hands for the anger was making his hands shake.

As the invader finished peeing he knelt beside the flower bed under the south window. The bed was filled with color. Wild iris, delphiniums, night-flowering stock and a mass of calendula. For a couple of seconds the soldier with the Mauser paused, stunned by the glory of his own garden. The invader was crouching by the bed, his back to the muzzle of the Mauser.

The soldier shouted a curse that meant he wished on the man an eternal torment in hell. It was a terrible curse, but it was also a warning. The invader stood quickly and turned.

Even as he stood facing the Mauser, still in the shadows, the soldier saw his revolver come up and aim across the stream straight at him. He squeezed the trigger of the powerful Mauser and the invader fell instantly, twisting on his face in the earth in his death throes. As soon as he was still, the soldier waded across the stream, the Mauser ready to fire again. But the man did not move. As he turned the body over to look into the face, the sunlight hit the wall inflaming the garden. He looked at the blood coming from the man's ear. Then he stood up again, replacing the Mauser, a sigh of satisfaction whistling through his teeth.

Stepping back, his boot hit the man's hand and he saw clenched tightly in it, the makeshift trowel he had fashioned, and he realized what he had done. He had killed the second gardener. The invader had been tending the very garden he had created, and he had shot his own second gardener dead.

He dropped to his haunches and put his head in his hands wondering what he should do next.

from *Scattered Psalms by Jacqueline Osherow*

XII. (At the Galleria dell'Accademia: Psalm 51)

Lord, open my lips, and my mouth will tell your praise.

Is that what he's saying? You can't be sure—
And this isn't the usual stance of prayer;
Still, it's what I hear as I look at him—
Not that he requires any psalm—
But here they all are, as yet unwritten:
The cedars whole, the mountains motionless,
The oceans' hands unruffled by applause
And stirring anxiously within the stone
Their soon to be discovered hallelujahs . . .

I say the slingshot is a metaphor,
That if there's any sign of a Goliath here
It's that once undifferentiated block of stone,
Which seemed to utter, from its holy mountain:
Cleanse me with hyssop and I shall be clean
(After Bathsheba, the psalm says, the ordeal with Nathan,
But this David is clearly thinking of Jonathan)
Wash me; I'll be whiter than snow
And he is, except for a disintegrating toe

Left to stand too long in the open air—
Which, with the softness of his open face—
Makes him look peculiarly defenseless;
He doesn't really seem like any warrior
Though I used to think I saw ferocity
In his profile (his full face held the poetry);
Now I see it's all diffused by awe
And the still unsorted out intensity
That hasn't yet come up with *hallelujah*

Or calculated what it takes to climb
The as yet uncharted mountain of the Lord;
Only Michelangelo has figured
That out. But when you look across the room
You see that his solution didn't last;
He grew impatient with his own perfection—
As if he switched allegiances to Samson,
Wanting not mere giants, but a whole foundation,
Even if it meant that he, too, would be lost—

And gave up easy strength to excavate
Some dim volcanic memory in the stone.
Was it worth it? The David's more famous
But think of what it took to call away
A face like Matthew's from that unhewn stone—
Or for these prisoners to smuggle out
Even a hint of torso, shoulder, thigh . . .
Each is a definitive self-portrait,
More accurate, surely, than the Nicodemus,

Who grieves above Christ dying down the street
With a pieced-together misproportioned arm.
Maybe it's just Christ's arm he's grieving for;
Michelangelo smashed it with a hammer
(He still required perfection; I was wrong)
But after his death, someone mended it
And, from many angles, it's sublime,
Though Michelangelo was right; the arm's too long.
Who knows? Perhaps he worried about the psalm:

Eyes they have, but they see not; ears they have . . .
He'd meant the Pietà for his own grave
But who was he to give God's son an arm?
Or, maybe, old now, he'd reread each psalm
And realized he'd even gotten David wrong—
This boy would never cry: *Oh Lord, how long?*
Or notice *the groaning of a prisoner*

Even across a room—gasping for air?
Or prying lips apart to mouth a prayer?

IX. (Looking out the Window: Psalm 121)

I will lift my eyes to the mountains, where my help will come; my help from God who makes heaven and earth.

Was it Jonathan Edwards who'd repeat, continually,
One verse from the Song of Songs for an entire day?
I am the rose of Sharon, the lily of the valley

He believed that, in the repetition,
He could hear Christ's voice replace his own.
And while a god who'd use that kind of self-description

Would put me off—mine asks sarcastic questions
Like *Where were you when I laid earth's foundations?*—
I'm also given to wild expectations.

Here's my secret: help does come
When you invoke it with the hills or even hum
The melody for that one bit of psalm.

It's the sheer idea of lifting up your eyes,
The heady speculation that the mountains rise
Purely for the sake of lifting us.

As if the endless business of creation
Required even our participation.
But wouldn't we know it? It's a wild notion,

Besides, it's no mean trick to lift your eyes
And I've been making an untenable promise
In my impatience to repeat the phrase

That requires nothing of me: *help will come*—
It *is* an extraordinary claim—
I will lift my eyes to the mountains—pure momentum

Could make anything happen after that—
Unless it's part of a triumvirate:
Lifted eyes, my help, the mountains' height—

Approximations for the undiluted
And various emergences of God,
A little like gas and liquid and solid

Versions of something wholly without substance.
But then—is it my failing?—there is a chance
That all I'll know of real deliverance

Is these blue-white mountains out my window
Still reeling from this morning's blast of snow.
They're uncannily beautiful without the Hebrew

So why don't I leave well enough alone?
Surely it's enough: a diamond-studded mountain.
Why insist on making it a stand-in

For what, if we could lift our eyes, we'd see?
(What help do I need? What is wrong with me?)
A lifted eye, a lily of the valley.

Eric LeMay

Eschatology

Niccolò Machiavelli, 1469–1527

Niccolò is restless in his bed. He wants
to run, wants to cut out over the humped
Italian countryside while the fields are still
barren with harvest, the soil black and spent.

He imagined his father's passage this way,
a disease of the spirit as a motion,
as a slapping of his boots against the earth.
No child's calling, no woman's, could sustain him.

But the men who surround him now want stories,
words for the tavern, words for their sons
whom Niccolò knows will amount to little.

So he begins to speak of two discrete lines
out of this world, one holds the ragged throng,
the other but a few men of greatness,

one leads to heaven, the other hell, though Niccolò
will not disclose which goes where. He imagines
a rough, ensuing wind. He wants to move.

Thomas Hobbes, 1588–1679

Down the hall, the nobility speculates:
supposed atheist, near-heretic, surely now
at the tag end of ninety-odd winters,
of death pressing through like rankweed, this man

will call for God. The Bishop of Chester
stands ready. Hobbes, however, left mute from a stroke,
does not raise his mottled hand. Could he speak,
he would mention his unconcern for dust

and a game he pursued in childhood
on those summer evenings when his mother,
in her silent house, did not need him.

Bird-nesting among the finest branches,
he'd wrap his hands around the brown, flecked eggs,
each heavy with its yolk, and slide them

in his pocket. To drain the shell, he'd pierce
both tips—the needle's point sufficing—
then place his mouth over one end, then blow.

John Locke, 1632–1704

Remembrance of dusted snows, of the manner
in which the girls adorned the parlor chairs,
their dresses like the pale shades of some river
frozen before a storm and pulled apart,

of the manner in which his charge leaned
against the mantel later that evening,
not a quiver in his stance, and inquired
whether or no Locke had found him a bride—

a lifetime ago, as if the bent woman
reading psalms to him now could have been
among those hopefuls, a silk napkin crushed

in her hands. Locke cannot muster, cannot
remember a passion for her blockish form,
her unsteady voice, and he wants to.

Beyond the window, the absolute blue
of the sky fills him with hope. Spring arrives
early. The cloud of his body ascends.

Marquis de Sade, 1740–1814

Sade knows pain and the affectations
of a ghostly muse. Before he sleeps,
her deep, feminine murmurs begin,
her voice, her dark fantasia, becoming

his own. He pens her words in minute script
on paper salvaged from the bits of kindling,
and later rolls them into tight, airless scrolls
which he conceals in the faulty mortar

of his cell. Thus the Bastille walls hum
with imagined cries, and the brittle moon
shivers in its revolutionary light.

Sade, still thirty years from death, believes
his muse will keep him satisfied, if not sated,
that she will remain forever enthralled

by his missives, but she is pure spirit
and too far removed from the blunt pleasures
of her skin to listen, to answer him.

Friedrich Nietzsche, 1844–1900

The asylum, the well-starched spectators
ushered in by his sister for a fee.
A lock of hair? But what to do with it?
One visitor fills his unscrewed pen-cap.

Cradling Friedrich's palm between her own,
his sister breathes too quickly in her blouse.

She mentions syphilis, degeneration,
intimates the greater of sins made flesh.

She has seduced him, she and her mother,
once believing no love could be condemned
or consumed or stopped. Now Friedrich seeks

only the lost heat of her and lies beside her
as he will when he dies, inconsolable.
Elizabeth knows he followed a woman

enough to share her with another man,
knows he'd follow still. So much cannot occur
in couples—betrayal, ridicule, love's worth.

Michel Foucault, 1926–1984

Like the tile-work spread beneath his feet
at the École Normale Supérieure,
where, unclothed, glasses sweating, Michel
stalked him through the night's aberrant hours,

like the etchings of Goya's war
hung on his dormitory wall, rendering
other fear beyond compare, their figures
prostrate on the ground, wrenched within lines,

his lover, at the head of the procession,
pinches his temples, envisions Michel
crouched above a lectern, straying deeper

into the histories of punishment.
His lover's eyes go closed, pressures of the street,
of sleeplessness, inside them, his fingers

press against his temple, as if to hold
whatever might give, as if each uncertain step
carried him from this world into the next.

Two Poems by George Bradley

Walking Philosophy

There are worlds, unwieldy, dreadful,
Difficult to grasp, just pick one up
And it grasps you, its grip of iron;

And there are sights, brochure-loads,
Wonders ancient and otherwise, but look
Too close and blur becomes confusion;

People, and they shrink from cultivation,
Beat retreats; facts, and the more you know
Of each the less you'll want to hang

On any, comes time for feet to dangle in the sky
While windswept clouds make blotchy patterns,
Gussy up some valley floor many feet below . . .

Patterns, yes, and the multiples thereof,
But they must come to you, haply
As rays picking up earth's gravitation,

Must find you staring into space, puttering
In the yard, out walking, aimless and amazed.
The unwasted life has not been lived.

Immigration of the Bodysnatchers

They arrived and were so beautiful, it was sad
They refused to snatch you, too, the aliens.
Teenage warriors resplendent in their fatigues,

Callow refugees of a conflict not given you
To understand, replete though it ever be
With disputed borders and the requisite enmities,

With the usual appalling bloodletting
And inadequate measures of relief,
They appeared in your hometown

And signed-on for the next campaign.
Nonchalant tacticians, plugged into the mumble
Of a culture between languages and rapt

In the comparison of monochrome tattoos,
They succeeded in surrounding you
Without paying much attention, although

They paused now and then to glance your way
And sometimes mingled indifference with your need.
It was touching, of course, and annoying

And soon over, for now they must move on again
To their idea of love, grunting and gesticulating,
Cunning in their not quite random remarks—

Protective coloration for a forest in which you
Find no repast—and so carry the sprawl forward
In all its ripeness and decay, slick under its sun,

Bound for that pitiless display of affection
That will clutch them by and by as the centaur's
Bloodstained cloak, but which for the nonce

Dawns as a splendor they alone decode
Gazing into glory holes, the abundant fire
And animal glitter of one another's eyes.

John Latta

Elogio di Frank O'Hara

Now that I am up here in the sky I can see
The *mare di San Tommaso* is a puddle of ink,
A hierarchy of imperial blue tints, tempting
The way order often is. No stranger's foot
Weighs on my heart and the earth today, howsoever
Cloud-begrudged and fickle, is turning
Itself "to" the unbudging sun though we're slow
To end our geocentric habits of three meddlesome centuries
Of science leading us by the dirty hand and do not desist
In saying the sun "rises," inexpert with the language
That exists merely to placate our sensibilities,
Troubled by the evacuations of art, how it leaves
Adamant puddles in the landscape that go to work
On the imaginations of stragglers like you and me.
You got through it all through pure charm,
Like a little grinning quark, knowing bravado
To be as specious as any other absolute, dashing
Naked into the night-stormy ocean, the only man awake
On earth and nobody left up to play with.
If we make our own suspicious amusements up and leave
Too many things undone it's because life is a work-
In-progress like any work is, always open and remaining so.
So it transpires that we must needs fill somebody's shoes
With feet of clay, feet broken off a statue
We've been lugging around on our shoulders
For a number of decades now not knowing
Exactly where to put it, in the kitchen or out
In the dreary afternoons of Vaughn Williams and rain
And a caravansary of words all leaking largesse, ambassadors
Of a perception that arrives in pieces, the way

A walk up along the ridge above Fiesole
Makes the path drop away, invisible
As the angels, the spectators, the sky-
Borne millions though we see now how the path continues
As descent and know it and we and they and you are there.

Two Poems by Elizabeth Weaver

Two Delicious, With Prawn Sauce

Rapunzel had her hair. All she had
was a phone she couldn't dial out on
and a second set of sheets—twin-sized
(meaning too short to reach the ground)
and they were in the wash.

And the phone calls: wrong numbers, hangups, letdowns.
If the words were foreign, she'd go by the tone;
if it sounded of insult, she all but broke
the phone with a slam. The answer to a question,
as a rule, was always yes. She was in love

with the quiet one who spoke Cantonese
inside the seductive static. Every night, a gingery
gift left outside the door, wrapped in foil.
Every note, a single lucky sentence.

The Cocoon

She stumbled on it. The story
had wrapped itself around her so long,
tapping and typing its coy music, that finally

it woke her, loosed her from the warm, numb towels,
and she remembered: She had been alive as recently
as Saturday, with exactly two arms, two lungs, unfurled.

She had known all the words. But what was this
design on her sides, spots over orange papier-mâché
stamped there by her own two tongues?

Beside her, deep in the pillows, she recognized
him: sleeping man forgiven, to be found later
beside her, woman who lives inside the cracks.

It would never do. It shouldn't have happened.
She had read it in the previous night's soup:
always there was one

on the wrong side of death,
always the drawer of knives
and the thousand days.

George Jay O'Leary

Midwestern Foundation Myth

A cunning oracle withholds the best.
The tax on prophecy is not to tell
the founder of a city how his sister
became a cow, the very beast he wanted,
in his ignorance, to sacrifice to the god
who had raped her with bullish abandon.

The usual obstacles delayed her fate.
A serpent devoured the founder's noisy men,
so appeasing gods or laying out broad avenues
had to wait. He sowed the serpent's teeth
like kernels of corn. The newly germinated
brothers ran each other through with spears.

Five were left. They skewered bull snakes
in their root cellars; ripped open
the prairies with plows of molded steel;
razed silos and barns; routed the main line
and spurs. They even strung a telegraph wire
so the coast could hear of their disasters.

Serpentine freight trains with slatted cars
hauled thousands of head to the market town.
They wound through the wooden labyrinth to feed
the slaughterhouses already bulging with slabs,
salted or on ice, since the first unblemished
heifer wandered onto that Great Plain.

Roderick Townley

Moonrise at Ashcroft

for WT

Silver crashed and the lights went out in Ashcroft.
A century passes in a dream.
Some houses stand,

some sink in cellar holes—gooseberry bushes
planted by pie-loving prospectors
mark where they stood,

tufts in the clefts of fields. Only night
is the same, the arguing stream
shadowed by the same

humped mountain. This is what old Jack Leahy,
the town's ghost poet, heard
from the stump on his porch

while he waited for moonrise: the cuffing breeze,
the ceaseless moil of water, hushing
and shouting at once.

This is the hour. The wind dies. The mountain's
shoulder glows. A shadow
begins its retreat

down Main Street like a coverlet slipping
from a bed. Now sudden
brightness flares

over the peak, glazing the meadow, the leaves
of a hundred thousand aspens
on the opposite slope,

the roofs of the Hotel View and blacksmith's shop.
Click off the flashlight. Write
on the silver page.

Two Poems by Susan Kinsolving

Dailies & Rushes

As a stunted woman (you might say
stunt) my body is every day
ready to explode in some crazy way.
My breasts feel wired, patched with squibs.
I'll take bruises, cuts, a few cracked ribs.
Ready for jumps, rolls, even ad-libs,
I want some action, to get real hot.
Stars get millions, but I'll take squat.
Falling into flames, I cry "Why? Why not?"

Sequins

What I wear, wears on you so darkly.
In spangled light,
I am recondite.
Bright discs of color satisfy my skin,
ornament this surface of self and flash a million meteors
across your dusty mirror. These are my mermaid's scales
for which I weighed the worth of my worn dress. Yes,
these tiny gaudy gleams are why I shed my sensible
shoes and pointed my toes to fit the dazzling idea
of this tale. Shimmering in this rare reflective glare,
I hear the siren who has come to alarm and enlighten you.
Call this cheap costuming or an epidermal illusion
full of foolishness, but know that something in this sheen
is suiting me. Cell by cell, this change wears well. Sequin
by sequin, beware of how I glisten
and what I wear.
Beware . . .

Mary Jane Nealon

Accident, Bedtime

Once upon a time I loved your rectum
as well as your ear, your skin took on
the majesty of feather when you spread
your arms above me, the pulse of your heart
abandoned for the sticky corners of my mouth.

Once upon a time I loved your back
as well as your testicles and burrowed there
until only my head remained above the skin,
gasping for air. The breezes that came in the room
paused above us, then became wind, then typhoon
until, swept into a rain cloud of our moisture,
we made weather look foolish.

Once upon a time I loved your prehistoric buttocks
as much as I loved your tongue, as much as your thighs
and so, insane almost with the outline of your body
and the texture of your hair, I slid into the swamp of you,
willingly, yet blinded by mud and tall grasses.
Then you crashed and the crazy wet sheets
tortured me with their big stains and musty smell.
It was that fast, the way the story ended,
no witch, no flying monkeys, just the shattered windshield
and your body, crumpled against the tree,
forgetting everything, forgetting even my name.

Memories of My Father, Alfred Kazin

Cathrael Kazin

I was so used to seeing his name in print that at first the obituaries did not faze me—the only odd feature was that new tag line, "dies at 83." He had always seemed to me most fully alive, most present, in print. In person, especially in the last years of his life, he was often heartbreakingly unreachable. He seemed always to be across high water, shouting from across a great divide. "Come here," he would beckon, only to bellow, if I finally made it, "Why did you take so long? Why are you such a mess?" or even, "Why do you never come?"

No one who loved him—and there were many of us—would have called him anything but difficult. He could be comically, professionally difficult—traveling a rapid circuit from reproachful to accusing, aggressive to indifferent. At such moments—and I confess that there were many of them—I would

© Jill Krementz

Alfred Kazin in 1997.

often seek solace in his books. He was so brilliant a student of his own loneliness that surely his dense defensiveness could be penetrated, no? After all, that extraordinary man, that walker in the city, the New York Jew himself, was my father. It was easier when we were both younger. I suspect it helped that I looked like him. We would walk endlessly in Riverside Park, "doing Bach"—a dangerous game in which one person started a tune and the other improvised some kind of harmony. Often the results were disastrous, but sometimes surprising, evanescently triumphant. We sang a lot and indiscriminately—socialist standbys, spirituals I'd learned at Quaker summer camp, "Battle Hymn of the Republic." A Dalton classmate famously remarked, one night in 1968 when my father came to pick me up, "Katey's Daddy knows the 'Internationale'!"

He was not in any conventional sense "good with children," and was terribly disappointed to discover that the "Plato" I wanted for my birthday was not the Greek philosopher but Play Doh, colored clay. But the quality that enabled him, three days from dying, to ask his Filipina home-care attendant, "Have you read Faulkner?" was exactly what made it possible for him to take his young female child seriously. It would never have occurred to him that I was too young or female to have ideas.

Nor was he conventionally difficult. Though there were certain types he superficially resembled—grumpy old man, scholarly curmudgeon, absentminded professor—he had a core of sweetness, a desperate longing to connect, a wish for you that was impossible to resist. He lacked many conventional vices. He was un-self-important in many ways, had little sense of himself as a literary personage. He was completely content to type furiously in the midst of his often broken-into studio on Fourteenth Street. He was not pretentious, was unutterably, incurably himself.

In his final weeks he acquired a loopy tenderness I hadn't seen for many years. I'm sure he was terrified of not being able to write, worried about the book he would leave unfinished. Its title gave him a particular *méchant* pleasure—Jews: the Marriage of Heaven and Hell. He had me read most of it aloud, begged me to "be a pal" to his book. Perched unbearably in the hospital bed that took up much of the living room, he was full of questions, questions, questions, about his nurses, my life in Israel, words in Hebrew, what exactly was it that I did at work? Though bitterly anti-Israel for many years, he now dreamily described himself as "not religious, but a labor Zionist" and wondered if it wasn't fun, after all, to live in a country full of Jews?

Of the quarrels with others he made, finally, some sort of peace. Of the quarrel with himself he had always made poetry.

I miss him with all my broken heart.

On the Cover: Kenneth Noland

Karen Wilkin

Kenneth Noland's name is synonymous with a particular kind of American abstraction—one based on the potency of color, rooted in the belief that relationships of hues, like music, can directly and wordlessly stir our deepest emotional and intellectual reserves. Noland's name stands, too, for pictures with lucid, near-geometric formats—images that ring changes on frontal, symmetrical, deceptively simple compositions, brought to life by seductive color. Probably the best known of these are the Circle paintings—unabashedly beautiful concentric rings of disembodied hues—with which he first announced himself as a painter to be reckoned with, four decades ago.

Recently, Noland has returned to his circle format, after years of exploring other permutations, rather like the composer of an extended set of variations restating the theme that was his original point of departure. Noland's new Circles are still about color's ability to trigger infinite associations and affect emotions; they are still about the unpredictable resonance created by placing unnameable hues side by side. Like the best of his first versions of the motif, Noland's new Circle series includes paintings that seem constructed with ravishing colors that never existed before and never could exist, except in the context of the picture before us. Yet Noland's new Circles are not reprisals but rather complete reinventions of his initial statements of the theme, informed (or more accurately, transformed) by his experience of the past forty years. Only their similar formats link the two series.

Most striking in the new Circles is their intimacy and their physicality. Small in size, with richly inflected surfaces, they bear witness as much to the presence of the artist's hand as to his eye. Unlike the disembodied Circles of the 1960s, in which color seemed magically to have been willed into the canvas without the intervention of touch, Noland's new Circles make us intensely aware of the act of transferring pigment to a surface. Each ring of paint, whatever its expanse, not only has a different hue, but a different density, from transparent wash to thickly troweled impasto (which paradoxically is often translucent), all of which heightens the drama, broadening the picture's emotional spectrum. The small Circles pull us toward them with their intimate size and their complexity of incident—"like a still life," Noland says, surprisingly.

Or perhaps not so surprisingly. For all of his dependence on intuition and spontaneity in his process, Noland is a sophisticated, analytical artist fascinated by the nature of his discipline. "I've been more and more aware that abstract pictures like my first Circles kept viewers at a distance," he said recently. "They weren't about detail. They were allover." Their complex color relationships, like their nuanced play of extensions and intervals, required and rewarded long scrutiny, but their immaculate surfaces were equally weighted in all parts and so held spectators at an optimum viewing distance from which the entire image was revealed. By contrast, a traditional representational painting, such as a still life, with its multitude of incidents, its varied weighting and its diversity of fictive textures, could be approached in several ways. Like an abstraction, a representational painting could be read for its total, unifying structure, but unlike an abstraction, it could also be interrogated for smaller, more disjunctive pictorial events. "Abstract paintings didn't have the specific qualities of traditional paintings. A traditional painting could have more than one scale. I got interested in that and I tried to discover how abstraction could have that level of detail," Noland explains.

His new Circles address these issues. "It's touch that draws you up," Noland says. Visible evidence of how the painter's hand traveled over the surface not only invites us to approach closely, but makes it imperative that we do so. In some pictures, our eye moves over the delicate geography of the surface as though exploring a new kind of landscape. In others, clues to the history of the painting's evolution—fragments of drawing, roughly brushed zones of color, or floating strokes, like test patches—demand even closer study. The series is notable for its variety of moods and temperatures, or to extend the musical analogy, its wide range of keys and orchestrations. Some pictures depend on opulent, loaded contrasts, lush build-ups of surface and staccato oppositions of intense color, while others are serene, sparse, contemplative, and so delicately adjusted that they threaten to dissolve into tinted haze. In some, the center is acknowledged or emphasized, while others stress the extension of the bands across the entire canvas. And so on. The differences between the intimate little Circle paintings, in fact, seem more notable than the similarities of their shared format.

For Noland's immediate forebears, the Abstract Expressionists of the forties and fifties, arriving at a signature image seemed essential to declaring oneself a serious artist. (Cynics would say that a signature image made it easier to identify a given artist.) For this generation, a particular way of putting a picture together was assumed to offer insight into its maker, as unwilled visible evidence of a particular personality.

For Noland, one of the generation of "cool" abstract painters who matured in the late fifties and early sixties, working with serial, repeated formats, such as his "signature" Circle, has a different basis. Stabilizing a few compositional givens permits him to give free rein to both his inventiveness and his thrift. It allows him to explore the last conceivable possibility of a fruitful idea and, more important, since he does not have to create a new structure for each painting, it permits him to concentrate on other, more subtle issues—of color, scale, interval, and visual weight, and the expressive possibilities of all of these elements. And it allows him to court the unexpected, since the repeated layout of the series both accentuates and cancels similarities, making the differences between pictures more telling for both the viewer and their maker.

Noland has long believed implicitly that "art comes from the work. I have to work things out by painting them," he says. "I can't just imagine what will happen. I have to do it and see it." It's neither overstatement nor oversimplification to say that his recent Circle pictures are like a diary of everything Noland has discovered in his working lifetime—about perception, about materials, about the nature of abstract painting itself.

NOTES ON CONTRIBUTORS

FICTION

Jon Billman is a sled-dog handler who lives in Wyoming. His work has appeared in such publications as *Zoetrope* and *Outside*, and a collection of his stories, *When We Were Wolves*, is forthcoming from Random House. He is working on a novel.

Robert Coover has won fellowships from the Rockefeller Foundation, the Guggenheim Foundation and the National Endowment for the Arts and has been the recipient of the William Faulkner Award, the American Academy of Arts and Letters Award and other honors. His works of fiction include *John's Wife*, *Pinocchio in Venice*, *The Public Burning*, *Gerald's Party* and *Briar Rose*. He lives in London and in Providence, Rhode Island, where he teaches at Brown University. His most recent novel is *Ghost Town*.

Michael Jacot has published nine novels, including *The Last Butterfly* and *An Emerald for Eamanja*. His new novel, *The Inner Temple Murders*, will appear this summer.

Julie Orringer received her MFA from the University of Iowa in 1996. She received the *Yale Review* Editors Prize for 1998. The story that appears in this issue won *The Paris Review* Discovery Prize for 1998.

CHRONICLE

Annie Dillard is the author of ten books, including *Holy the Firm*, *An American Childhood*, *The Writing Life*, *The Living* (a novel) and *Pilgrim at Tinker Creek*, which was awarded the Pulitzer Prize for nonfiction in 1975. Her latest book, *For the Time Being*, a section of which appears in this issue, will be published by Knopf in the spring.

POETRY

George Bradley is the author of three books of poetry, the most recent of which is *The Fire Fetched Down*. He edited *The Yale Younger Poets Anthology, 1998*. He lives in Chester, Connecticut.

Matthew Greenfield teaches renaissance poetry and drama at Bowdoin College. His poems have appeared in such journals as *Tikkun*, *Raritan*, *Western Humanities Review* and *Southwest Review*.

Beth Gylys has a Ph.D. in creative writing and literature from the University of Cincinnati.

Susan Kinsolving's new book of poems, *Dailies & Rushes*, will be published this year. She has taught at California Insitute of the Arts and the University of Connecticut. Yaddo, Ragdale and the Connecticut Commission on the Arts have awarded her fellowships.

John Latta's first collection, *Rubbing Torsos*, was published in 1979. His poems appear in a number of journals, including *The Gettysburg Review* and *The Iowa Review*.

Eric LeMay's work has appeared in *The Georgia Review* and *Antioch Review*. He lives in Chicago.

Anne McCarty graduated in June from the MFA program at Bennington College. She writes and teaches in Cincinnati.

Honor Moore's *The White Blackbird: A Life of the Painter Margarett Sargeant by her Granddaughter* will be out in paperback this summer. She is completing a new book of poems.

Joan Murray's prizewinning collection, *Looking for the Parade*, and her book-length verse narrative, *Queen of the Mist*, will both be published this spring.

Mary Jane Nealon is a poet and a registered nurse. She was a poetry fellow at the Fine Arts Center in Provincetown 1995–1997. Her first book, *Rogue Apostle*, is forthcoming.

George Jay O'Leary received his MFA from the University of Florida and now lives in Otego, New York. His work has appeared in *Southwest Review*.

Kim Mattson received her MFA from Columbia University in 1996.

Jacqueline Osherow's fourth book of poems, *Dead Men's Praise*, will appear this spring.

Christopher Patton recently received a grant from the Canada Council to complete his first book of poems. He lives in Vancouver, British Columbia.

John Reibetanz has published four books of poetry. His fifth book, *Mining for Sun*, will appear in 1999.

David St. John is the author of nine collections of poetry, including the forthcoming *In the Pines: Lost Poems 1972–1997* and *The Red Leaves of Night*. He is editor-at-large of *Antioch Review*.

Sherod Santos's fourth collection of poems, *The Pilot Star Elegies*, will appear this winter. The poem that appeared in this issue received the 1998 Bernard F. Conners Prize from *The Paris Review*.

Reginald Shepherd is the author of two collections of poetry, *Some Are Drowning* and *Angel, Interrupted*. His third book, *Wrong*, will appear this spring.
Roderick Townley is the editor of *Night Errands: How Poets Use Dreams* and author of eight other books. The 1998 winner of the Peregrine Prize for short fiction, he lives in Kansas.
William Wadsworth was a 1997 MacDowell Colony Fellow in Poetry. He is the executive director of The Academy of American Poets in New York City.
David Wagoner's *Traveling Light: Collected Poems, 1958–1998* will be published this spring. He edits *Poetry Northwest* for the University of Washington.
V.S.M. Wang has studied English at Harvard College, attended Columbia Law School, worked in a Manhattan law firm, and obtained a master's degree in English at the University of Virginia. She now works in a law firm in San Jose.
Elizabeth Weaver is an MFA candidate in the writing division of Columbia University's School of the Arts in New York City. She also works full time as an editorial assistant and has started a creative writing workshop for patients at St. Luke's Hospital.

INTERVIEWS

Donzelina Barroso (José Saramago interview) is program coordinator of the Camões Center for the study of the Portuguese-speaking world and editor of the *Camões Center Quarterly* at Columbia University. Her articles and essays have been published in the newspaper *Jornal Luso-Americano* newspaper, and the publications of the Newark Museum and the New Jersey Performing Arts Center, among others. She lives in New York City and Lisbon.
Willard Spiegelman (Charles Tomlinson interview) is the Hughes Professor of English at Southern Methodist University and editor of the *Southwest Review*. His latest book is *Majestic Indolence*.

ART

Ilya Kabakov is represented by the Barbara Gladstone Gallery. **Anthony Haden-Guest** is the author of *The Last Party: Studio 54 and the Culture of the Night* as well as *True Colors: the Real Life of the Art World*.
Kcho (Alexis Leyva Machado) is represented by the Barbara Gladstone Gallery. All images appear courtesy of Barbara Gladstone Gallery. Photo credit © Zindman/Fremont.
Richard Basil Mock lives in Brooklyn, New York.
Kenneth Noland's work was recently exhibited by the Andŕe Emmerich Gallery. **Karen Wilkin**'s latest book is *Morandi*.

The Paris Review

is pleased to announce
our 1998 prizewinners

Will Self

has been awarded

The Aga Khan Prize for Fiction

for his story in issue 146,
"Tough Tough Toys for Tough Tough Boys"

The B.F. Conners Prize for Poetry

has been awarded to

Neil Azevedo

for his poem in issue 148,
"Caspar Hauser Songs"

and

Sherod Santos

for his poem in issue 149,
"Elegy For My Sister"

Julie Orringer

has been awarded

The Paris Review Discovery Prize

for her story in issue 149,
"When She Is Old and I Am Famous"

UNITED STATES POSTAL SERVICE™

Statement of Ownership, Management, and Circulation

(Required by 39 USC 3685)

1. Publication Title	2. Publication Number	3. Filing Date
THE PARIS REVIEW	0 0 3 1 - 2 0 3 7	9/18/98
4. Issue Frequency	**5. Number of Issues Published Annually**	**6. Annual Subscription Price**
QUARTERLY	4	$34.00
7. Complete Mailing Address of Known Office of Publication *(Not printer) (Street, city, county, state, and ZIP+4)*		**Contact Person**
45-39 171 PLACE FLUSHING NY 11358		LILLIAN VON NICKERN
		Telephone
		718 539 7085

8. Complete Mailing Address of Headquarters or General Business Office of Publisher *(Not printer)*

AS ABOVE

9. Full Names and Complete Mailing Addresses of Publisher, Editor, and Managing Editor *(Do not leave blank)*

Publisher *(Name and complete mailing address)*

DRUE HEINZ 541 EAST 72 ST NEW YORK NY 10021

Editor *(Name and complete mailing address)*

GEORGE A PLIMPTON 541 EAST 72 ST., NEW YORK NY 10021

Managing Editor *(Name and complete mailing address)*

DANIEL KUNITZ 541 EAST 72 ST., NEW YORK NY 10021

10. Owner *(Do not leave blank. If the publication is owned by a corporation, give the name and address of the corporation immediately followed by the names and addresses of all stockholders owning or holding 1 percent or more of the total amount of stock. If not owned by a corporation, give the names and addresses of the individual owners. If owned by a partnership or other unincorporated firm, give its name and address as well as those of each individual owner. If the publication is published by a nonprofit organization, give its name and address.)*

Full Name	Complete Mailing Address
THE PARIS REVIEW INC.,	45-39 171 PLACE FLUSHING NY 11358
GEORGE A PLIMPTON	541 EAST 72 ST., NEW YORK NY 10021
PETER MATTHIESSEN	BRIDGE LN., SAGAPONACK NY 11962
THOMAS GUINZBURG	39 EAST 67 ST., NEW YORK NY 10021

11. Known Bondholders, Mortgagees, and Other Security Holders Owning or Holding 1 Percent or More of Total Amount of Bonds, Mortgages, or Other Securities. If none, check box → ☒ None

Full Name	Complete Mailing Address

12. Tax Status *(For completion by nonprofit organizations authorized to mail at special rates) (Check one)*
The purpose, function, and nonprofit status of this organization and the exempt status for federal income tax purposes:

☐ Has Not Changed During Preceding 12 Months

☐ Has Changed During Preceding 12 Months *(Publisher must submit explanation of change with this statement)*

PS Form **3526**, September 1995 *(See Instructions on Reverse)*

13. Publication Title THE PARIS REVIEW		14. Issue Date for Circulation Data Below 146 SPRING 1998	
15. Extent and Nature of Circulation		Average No. Copies Each Issue During Preceding 12 Months	Actual No. Copies of Single Issue Published Nearest to Filing Date
a. Total Number of Copies *(Net press run)*		10270	10910
b. Paid and/or Requested Circulation	(1) Sales Through Dealers and Carriers, Street Vendors, and Counter Sales *(Not mailed)*	5619	6196
	(2) Paid or Requested Mail Subscriptions *(Include advertiser's proof copies and exchange copies)*	2630	2509
c. Total Paid and/or Requested Circulation *(Sum of 15b(1) and 15b(2))* ▶		8249	8705
d. Free Distribution by Mail *(Samples, complimentary, and other free)*		198	184
e. Free Distribution Outside the Mail *(Carriers or other means)*		303	300
f. Total Free Distribution *(Sum of 15d and 15e)* ▶		501	484
g. Total Distribution *(Sum of 15c and 15f)* ▶		8750	9189
h. Copies not Distributed	(1) Office Use, Leftovers, Spoiled	960	1721
	(2) Returns from News Agents	560	N/A
i. Total *(Sum of 15g, 15h(1), and 15h(2))* ▶		10270	10910
Percent Paid and/or Requested Circulation *(15c / 15g x 100)*		94	95

16. Publication of Statement of Ownership
☒ Publication required. Will be printed in the FALL #148 issue of this publication.
☐ Publication not required.

17. Signature and Title of Editor, Publisher, Business Manager, or Owner: Lillian von Nickern, bus. mgr — Date: 9/18/98

I certify that all information furnished on this form is true and complete. I understand that anyone who furnishes false or misleading information on this form or who omits material or information requested on the form may be subject to criminal sanctions (including fines and imprisonment) and/or civil sanctions (including multiple damages and civil penalties).

Instructions to Publishers

1. Complete and file one copy of this form with your postmaster annually on or before October 1. Keep a copy of the completed form for your records.
2. In cases where the stockholder or security holder is a trustee, include in items 10 and 11 the name of the person or corporation for whom the trustee is acting. Also include the names and addresses of individuals who are stockholders who own or hold 1 percent or more of the total amount of bonds, mortgages, or other securities of the publishing corporation. In item 11, if none, check the box. Use blank sheets if more space is required.
3. Be sure to furnish all circulation information called for in item 15. Free circulation must be shown in items 15d, e, and f.
4. If the publication had second-class authorization as a general or requester publication, this Statement of Ownership, Management, and Circulation must be published; it must be printed in any issue in October or, if the publication is not published during October, the first issue printed after October.
5. In item 16, indicate the date of the issue in which this Statement of Ownership will be published.
6. Item 17 must be signed.

Failure to file or publish a statement of ownership may lead to ension of second-class authorization.

The Paris Review
Booksellers Advisory Board

THE PARIS REVIEW BOOKSELLERS ADVISORY BOARD is a group of owners and managers of independent bookstores from around the world who have agreed to share with us their knowledge and expertise.

Available now from the Flushing office
BACK ISSUES OF THE PARIS REVIEW

No.	18	Ernest Hemingway Interview; Giacometti Portfolio; Philip Roth Fiction.	$25.00
	25	Robert Lowell Interview; Hughes Rudd, X.J. Kennedy.	10.00
	30	S.J. Perelman and Evelyn Waugh Interviews; Niccolo Tucci, 22 poets.	10.00
	35	William Burroughs Interview; Irvin Faust, Leonard Gardner, Ron Padgett.	10.00
	37	Allen Ginsberg and Cendrars Interviews; Charles Olson, Gary Snyder.	10.00
	44	Creeley and I.B. Singer Interviews; James Salter, Diane di Prima.	15.00
	45	Updike Interview; Hoagland Journal; Veitch, Brautigan, Padgett, O'Hara.	10.00
	46	John Dos Passos Interview; Thomas M. Disch, Ted Berrigan, Kenneth Koch.	10.00
	47	Robert Graves Interview; Ed Sanders, Robert Creeley, Tom Clark.	10.00
	62	James Wright Interview; Joe Brainard, Christo Portfolio.	10.00
	63	J.P. Donleavy and Steinbeck Interviews; Louis Simpson, Robert Bly.	10.00
	64	Kingsley Amis and P.G. Wodehouse Interviews; Diane Vreuls, Thomas M. Disch.	10.00
	66	Stanley Elkin Interview; Richard Stern, W.S. Merwin.	10.00
	67	Cheever and Wheelock Interviews; Maxine Kumin, Aram Saroyan.	10.00
	68	William Goyen Interview; John Updike, William Stafford.	10.00
	69	Kurt Vonnegut Interview; William Burroughs, Ed Sanders, John Logan.	10.00
	70	William Gass Interview; Peter Handke, William S. Wilson, Galway Kinnell.	10.00
	72	Richard Wilbur Interview; Joy Williams, Norman Dubie.	10.00
	73	James M. Cain and Anthony Powell Interviews; Dallas Wiebe, Bart Midwood.	10.00
	74	Didion, Drabble and Oates Interviews; Vincente Aleixandre Portfolio; Max Apple.	10.00
	75	Gardner, Shaw Interviews; Handke Journal, Dubus, Salter, Gunn, Heaney.	10.00
	76	Ignatow, Levi, Rhys Interviews; Jean Rhys Memoir Louis Simpson.	10.00
	77	Stephen Spender Interview; Mark Strand, Joseph Brodsky, Philip Levine.	10.00
	78	Andrei Voznesensky Interview; Voznesensky/Ginsberg Conversation; Edie Sedgwick Memoir; T. Coraghessan Boyle, Tom Disch, Odysseus Elytis.	15.00
	79	25th ANNIVERSARY: R. West Interview; Paris Review Sketchbook; Hemingway, Faulkner, Southern, Gass, Carver, Dickey, Schuyler, Gellhorn/Spender/Jackson Letters.	15.00
	80	Barthelme, Bishop Interviews; Reinaldo Arenas, J.D. Salinger Feature.	10.00
	81	T. Williams, P. Bowles Interviews; Wiebe, Atwood, Federman Fiction; Montale Poetry.	20.00
	83	J. Brodsky, S. Kunitz Interviews; Gerald Stern/B.F. Conners Prize Poetry.	15.00
	84	P. Larkin, J. Merrill Interviews; T.C. Boyle, Edmund White Fiction.	15.00
	85	M. Cowley, W. Maxwell Interviews; H. Brodkey, Bill Knott Poetry.	15.00
	87	H. Boll, Infante Interviews; Milosz, C.K. Williams Poetry.	10.00
	88	Gordimer, Carver Interviews; Hill, Nemerov Poetry; McCourt, Davis Fiction.	10.00
	89	James Laughlin, May Sarton Interviews; F. Bidart Poetry, Zelda Fitzgerald Feature.	10.00
	90	John Ashbery, James Laughlin Interviews; C. Wright Poetry; E. Garber Fiction.	10.00
	91	J Baldwin, E. Wiesel Interviews; Morand, R. Wilson Fiction; Clampitt Poetry.	10.00
	92	M. Kundera, E. O'Brien, A. Koestler Interviews; E.L. Doctorow Fiction.	10.00
	93	30th ANNIVERSARY: Roth, Ionesco, Cortazar Interviews; Boyle Fiction; Brodsky, Carver Poetry.	15.00
	97	Hollander, McGuane Interviews; Dickey, Kosinski Features; Dixon Fiction, Wright Poetry.	15.00
	98	L. Edel, R. Stone Interviews; R. Stone Fiction; L. Edel Feature.	10.00
	99	A. Robbe-Grillet, K. Shapiro Interviews; E. Tallent Fiction; D. Hall Poetry.	10.00
	100	DOUBLE 100th: Hersey, Irving Interviews; Gordimer, Munro Fiction; Merrill, Milosz Poetry.	15.00
	105	Calisher, Gaddis Interviews; B. Okri Fiction; A. Zagajewski Poetry.	15.00
	106	35th ANNIV: Lessing, Yourcenar Interviews; C. Smith Fiction; Logue Poetry; Styron Feature.	15.00
	108	A. Hecht, E. White Interviews; C. Baxter, J. Kauffman Fiction; S. Olds Poetry.	10.00
	109	Mortimer, Stoppard Interviews; Burroughs, Minot Fiction; Mathews, Simic Poetry.	10.00
	111	Fowles, Fugard, Spencer Interviews; Tucci, Gurganus Fiction; Proust, Rilke Translations.	10.00
	112	Kennedy, Skvorecky Interviews; Malamud, Maspéro Fiction; Perec, Pinsky Poetry.	10.00
	114	Sarraute, Settle Interviews; Matthiessen, P. West Fiction; F. Wright Poetry.	10.00
	115	Murdoch, Stegner Interviews; Bass Fiction; Laughlin Poetry; Merwin Feature.	10.00
	116	Angelou, Vargas Llosa Interviews; Perec Fiction; Ashbery Poetry; Stein Feature.	10.00
	117	Atwood, Pritchett Interviews; R. Price, Stern Fiction; Kizer, Logue Poetry.	10.00
	118	Bloom, Wolfe Interviews; Tolstaya Fiction; Ashbery Poetry; Carver, Burgess Features.	10.00
	119	Grass, Paz Interviews; M. McCarthy Feature; DeMarinis Fiction; Bonnefoy, Hacker Poetry.	10.00
	120	Hall, Morris Interviews; Milosz Feature; Brodkey, Mailer Fiction; Corn, Lasdun Poetry.	10.00
	121	Brodkey, Price Interviews; Minot, West Fiction; Z. Herbert Poetry; D. Hall Feature.	10.00
	122	Amichai, Simon Interviews; Konrád Fiction; Montale, Zarin Poetry; Merrill Feature.	10.00
	123	Mahfouz Interview; J. Scott Fiction; Ashbery, Sarton Poetry; Schwartz-Laughlin Letters.	10.00
	124	Calvino, Paley Interviews; Grass, Johnson, Moore Fiction; Clampitt, Herbert Poetry.	10.00
	126	Clampitt, Helprin Interviews; J. Williams, Eco Fiction; Goldbarth, Zarin Poetry.	10.00
	127	Logue, Salter Interviews; Carroll, Shepard Fiction; Ammons, Swenson Poetry.	10.00
	128	40th ANNIVERSARY: DeLillo, Morrison Interviews; Canin, García Márquez Fiction; Graham, Merwin Poetry; Cheever, Hemingway, Pound Documents.	15.00
	129	Stafford Interview; J. Scott Fiction; Yenser Poetry; Salter, Trilling Features.	10.00
	130	Kesey, Snodgrass Interviews; Braverman, Power Fiction, Paz Poetry.	10.00
	131	Bonnefoy, Munro Interviews; Moody, Pritchard Fiction; Hacker, Merrill Poetry; Bishop-Swenson Letters.	10.00
	132	Auchincloss, Gottlieb Interviews; Gass, Thon, West Fiction; Kinnell Poetry; Kazin Feature.	10.00
	133	Achebe, Milosz Interviews; Byatt, D'Ambrosio Fiction; Hirsch, Wagoner Poetry.	10.00
	134	Hughes, Levi Interviews; Fischer, Schulman Fiction; Ammons, Kizer Poetry; Welty Feature.	10.00
	135	Gunn, P.D. James, O'Brian Interviews; DeMarinis, Mayo, Prose Fiction; Rich, Wright Poetry.	10.00
	136	HUMOR: Allen, Keillor, Trillin Interviews; Barth, Boyle Fiction; Clifton, Updike Poetry; Bloom Feature.	30.00
	137	Sontag, Steiner Interviews; Bass Fiction; Seshadri Poetry; Russian Feature.	10.00
	138	SCREENWRITING: Dunne, Price, Wilder Interviews; Diaz Fiction; Southern Feature.	10.00
	139	Ammons, Buckley, Cela Interviews; Davenport, Franzen Fiction; Kizer Poetry.	10.00
	140	Ford, Oz Interviews; Butler, Eakins Fiction; Bidart, Olds Poetry; Cooper Feature.	10.00
	141	Snyder, Vendler Interviews; New Fiction; New Poetry; Marquez Feature.	10.00
	142	THEATER: Mamet, Shepard, Wasserstein Interviews; McDonagh Play.	15.00
	143	Le Carré, Morris Interviews; Oates, Powell, Smith Fiction; Merwin Poetry; Salter Feature.	10.00
	144	Heaney, Pinsky Interviews; Moody, Wallace Fiction; Hacker, Szymborska Poetry.	10.00
	145	Rosset, Winterson Interviews; Millhauser, Richard Fiction; Hirsch Poetry.	10.00
	146	BRITAIN: Amis Interview; Byatt, Foden, Self Fiction; Armitage, Motion Poetry.	10.00
	147	Banks, Kadaré Interviews; Bass, Cooley, Knight Fiction; An Oulipo Sampler.	10.00
	148	Naipaul, Strand Interviews; de Bernières, Williams Fiction; Vonnegut Libretto; Hadas Poetry	10.00

Please add $3.00 for postage and handling for up to 2 issues; $4.75 for 3 to 5. Payment should accompany order. For orders outside the U.S. please double the shipping costs. Payments must be made in U.S. currency. Prices and availability subject to change. **Address orders to: 45-39 171 Place, Flushing, N.Y. 11358**

MASTERCARD/VISA # ______________________________ **EXP. DATE** __________

Petaluma
1st. Ave. at 73rd. St., New York City
772-8800